SONG OF A Thousand Seas

Song of a Thousand Seas

ZANA FRAILLON

UQP

First published 2025 by University of Queensland Press
PO Box 6042, St Lucia, Queensland 4067 Australia
Reprinted 2026

University of Queensland Press (UQP) acknowledges the Traditional Owners and their custodianship of the lands on which UQP operates. We pay our respects to their Ancestors and their descendants, who continue cultural and spiritual connections to Country. We recognise their valuable contributions to Australian and global society.

uqp.com.au
reception@uqp.com.au

Cover design by Stephanie Spartels
Cover and internal illustrations by Aviva Reed
Author photograph by Julian Fraillon
Typeset in 12/16 pt Adobe Caslon by University of Queensland Press
Printed in Australia by McPherson's Printing Group

Queensland Government

University of Queensland Press is supported by the Queensland Government through Arts Queensland.

Australian Government

Creative Australia

University of Queensland Press is assisted by the Australian Government through Creative Australia, its principal arts investment and advisory body.

A catalogue record for this book is available from the National Library of Australia.

ISBN 978 0 7022 6631 7 (pbk)
ISBN 978 0 7022 6823 6 (epdf)
ISBN 978 0 7022 6824 3 (epub)

University of Queensland Press uses papers that are natural, renewable and recyclable products made from wood grown in well-managed forests and other controlled sources. The logging and manufacturing processes conform to the environmental regulations of the country of origin.

FSC
www.fsc.org
MIX
Paper | Supporting responsible forestry
FSC® C001695

To the real Houdini and her amazing keeper and friend, Chelsea. Thank you for teaching me to speak Octopus.

Welcome to the reef!

Can you see who is lurking in this tank?
She has eight arms, three hearts, zero bones, thousands of suckers and is a master of disguise.
It's Houdini! Houdini is a day octopus (*Octopus cyanea*).

Animal type
Cephalopod

Habitat
Coral reefs

Diet
Crustaceans, molluscs and fish

Size
Up to 80 centimetres

Did you know?

Octopuses have NINE brains – one brain between their eyes and a smaller brain in each arm. This means that each arm can think on its own, and all the brains can also think together. No wonder octopuses are so smart!

Tank buddies

There is someone else in this tank too.
Can you see Spike, the eleven-armed sea star?
You can see more sea stars in the Touch Tank, located on Level 1.

Not welcome

Our nine Octopus brains have a lot we'd like
to say to the Waves of people who
come every day to stare to gawk to
squeak to squawk to squeal to bang on our glass –
we'd have a lot to say if only they
knew how to listen.
The first thing we'd say is

GO AWAY!

Early mornings

We are in the Weeds waiting
when Paul comes in all
keys jingle-jangling
footstomps thundering
flicking the lights at their switch – one, two, three – and
Good morning, Houdini, you grumpy old thing!
We wait. Turn ourselves to Stone and don't
ever say good morning back.

Our Den

We have all sorts of treasures
hidden in our Den and it's built just the way
that we like it. Under the Rocks with the
Weeds growing tall so all of the
people with eyes trying to spy us
don't know where to find us.
In our Den we like to think. To stash. To hide.
To watch. To ponder. To plan.

Patience

Paul called us Houdini when we were
very small and all of the tanks we were put in
were so easy to escape from. Paul thinks
the new tank stopped us. Paul thinks
the tube blowing bubbles through jets that
gets our skin all tingling with joy and the toys he gives
us each day to play with distract us from trying to escape.
But we are just very good at waiting.

Sea Star

Spike doesn't have a lot to say but she
is an excellent listener.
She's very very old and very very wise
and when we creep from our Den she
watches as though she is wanting to
come creeping come crawling come blooming
come bursting out with us.
Once, Spike says, *the whole world was Sea*.

Games

We wait in the Weeds for Paul to
come past then we blast him with spray from the
very coldest very deepest very darkest part of our tank.
Right through the mesh. It gets him every time.
It's a fun little game and his squeal and his
rage make our days in this cage drift by just
a little bit faster.
We ripple to green so he knows we are laughing.

School tours

Say hello to Houdini, everyone! Paul smiles and
shuffles the young ones closer.
Who can see Houdini back there? She likes to hide.
Some octopuses are shy, but Houdini is just grumpy!
Houdini came to us when she was very young.
In the wild, day octopuses live in coral reefs.
That's why we made her a reef here.
Who can see her? Anyone? Anyone at all?

Paul's fact

Most octopuses, Paul says,
like to hunt in the night.
But Houdini is a day octopus.
Day octopuses hunt at dawn and dusk.
That's why they are particularly good at
camouflage. They stalk crabs, clams and fish
and can change the colour and texture of their skin
so they blend in with the coral and rocks.

Our fact

We want to say that in the day *we*
do not hunt at all. The Sea is so very
big so very full but our tank is so
very small so
very empty.
Far too empty
far too small for
hunting.

People are.

And every day the people say
the same thing, noses pressed to the glass and they ask
Where is she? Knock knock knock.
Can't you make her come out? Bang bang bang.
What's the point if you can't see her? Tap tap tap.
Is there even an octopus in here? Slap slap slap.
Can we see something else now?
Octopuses are boring.

Aquariums

As Paul walks away we hear him say to those
young ones that aquariums are very important.
They let us see into a whole other world, he says.
They let us do research, he says.
Meeting an animal makes you care about them, he says.
And a young one sighs. ***But we didn't meet the octopus***.
Paul looks back at us peering from our Den and
Yes, well. That's Houdini for you.

People aquariums

We wonder then about people aquariums.
Where the people have to stay and the only way
they can breathe is if we
let them. And the Animals that would eat them must
watch them instead so they learn how to love them for
more than just their flavour.
Such places would be very popular.
If we lived in the Sea we would suggest it.

Questions

We ask Spike
Why are people?
and Spike, so old so wise so
sure, says

nothing at all.

It seems people are a kind of
puzzle
known only to themselves.

Spike's fact

Earth
Spike says
is 70 per cent
water.
People
Spike says
are 70 per cent
water too.

Just like us

People live on the Land and forget
that they carry the Sea deep inside them.
Waves and Tides that whoosh under their skin –
we hear the water feel the water smell
the water carried within and the
rhythm of that flow lets us know that once
those people
came from the Sea too.

Dreaming

Sometimes we dream of being in the Sea.
Not Paul's Sea on the screen that's the same
every day never changing the way it is
going never changing its beat never changing the
heat that flows all the way through it.
That one is flat. Empty and dead like the
water in our tank. But in our dreams the Sea
she is fierce she is feral she is free.

Momentary fun

When the clock dings once
Paul comes and gives us some things to play with.
Puzzles and boxes with snacks deep inside and toys that
hide treats to munch on.
We know he does it so we don't feel so trapped like
our brains are too buzzed like our skin is too
small like we are all too empty.
They are fun for a bit we suppose.

Favourites

Of all the toys Paul brings us
the one we love best is Mr
Potato Head and we shred him piece by
piece shed his legs rip his hair his nose his lips and
give his eyes to Spike.
She carries them under her arms and
the young ones peering through the glass
go wild.

More momentary fun

When the clock dings three times Paul tries to tidy our
tank. With his trolley full of buckets and cloths, his
sponges on sticks and his tricks to try and distract us.
He vacuums our Stones and spits them out tasting all
wrong and fills in the pits we dug all morning long and
puts back our wood we yanked into a
better position. But we don't mind.
Stopping his tidying is fun for a bit too.

Waiting

The days are all the same and while we like
to play our games and squirt water at the lights so
they fizz-spark and turn dark or use Stones to block
the pipes so the water floods the floor and makes
Paul moan and roar with anger it
is the night that really excites us.
Days are for watching listening playing planning but
nights are for adventure.

Timing

When Paul first moved us to this tank he always
locked the lid – sealed, fastened and firm. Checked all the
edges all the hinges all the seams. Squeezed shut any gaps
any openings. *Don't want you escaping again*,
Paul said. *Can't afford to replace you*, he mumbled.
So we waited. Quiet in our Den. And slowly
Paul stopped being so careful.
People, it seems, are very easy to train.

See ya

Goodnight, girl, Paul says, shuts the lid tight
clicks the lock tight, taps it for luck – tap tap tap – but
doesn't check the edges like he used to. And Paul
doesn't know about the gap at the back where the hinge
has been wriggled undone.
A gap just big enough to squeeze an arm through.
Another arm. A head. Three hearts. 3,154 suckers and
six more arms. Our exit.

Nights

There is a heavy hush that falls when the halls are
all empty and Paul shuts the door behind him.
When the lights are all flicked and the locks
are all clicked. We wait with every sucker buzzing
every brain brimming blood bursting skin dancing
with what is to come.
We may not hunt like we should in the day but
the night is a different Beast.

Joe

We wait for Joe to come past with a mop in his hands
his ears full of music and his feet bursting to dance.
Houdini! My friend! He smiles and he laughs.
No adventures tonight, I hope.
Joe is a delight of the night and the taste
in the air whenever he is there is
the taste of
song and of happiness.

A different aquarium

At night everything is different and the whole aquarium
is ours. Just ours. We squeeze through our exit and
onto the floor and then we begin to
explore. Out from our room down the steps up the hall
past the walls of Fish of Turtles of Crabs all
swimming like they don't even know that
it is not the real Sea they are
living in.

Dinner

Who
we wonder
will we have for dinner tonight?
And the sight of them swimming not knowing
we are growing closer not seeing us as
we crawl across the floor through the door and up and into
their tank thrills us and fills us with unbound delight.
Tonight we think we will pay a visit to the Flounder …

Sea

We feel her. The Sea.
If we cross over the floor and through the
arched door with the boat painted bright above it
and crawl our way right to the very   edge
press up tight to the wall then the Sea
she ripples through our skin like Sunshine.
Like the music Joe plays when he dances, his smile lit up
like the memory of morning.

Paul's Den

Paul has all sorts of treasures
hidden in his Den and it's built just the way
that he likes it. But
Paul doesn't know that his Den is where we
go when we are trying to find a new treasure.
Tonight we find his keys on the floor
and we know for sure that they are the
best treasure yet.

Maps

Every night we follow the path on the floor
exploring just a little bit more of the
aquarium. We are careful never to go too far to get
too dry to climb too high to always make it back but
tonight there's a sound we heard long before
and every single part of us wants to
needs to
aches to hear more.

Sea howl

The Sea she is singing she is howling so strong she is
calling us. Drifting her voice up up through the Waves
twirling and whirling up up
through the pipes up up through the drain
in the far washroom floor under the door and down
the long hall urging us all to follow.
Every part of us howls back
a silent cry too ancient to ignore.

Urge

The washroom is so so far but the
howl of that song is so so strong
waking up memories inside us
and we don't stop to wonder if we've been too long
out of water
we need to explore just a little bit more
need to get just a little bit closer
to that singing.

Oh.

We realise now that we may have made a
rather big
mistake.
The ground feels so sharp now our tank is too far now
and we are going too
s l o w
now to make it all the way back to our Den.
Everything is turning to grey.

Rescue?

And then there's the beat of Joe's feet on the floor
and we pour ourselves into his hands – so soft so sure
and he tastes of a thousand Sunrises.
There you are! I followed your trail and a good thing too.
Look at the state of you. Don't worry. I won't tell a soul.
He laughs. *Look at me! Keeping secrets with an octopus!*
Back you go. Forgive me. I know what it's like to be caged.
And we watch as his smile curls to nothing.

Late mornings

We are in the Weeds waiting
when Paul comes in all
jangling thundering flicking stomping and he has
a young one with him.
You can sit there and do your homework, Paul growls, his
voice gravel-dark, eyes hard like Rocks and
the young one sits. She waits. Turns herself to Stone
and doesn't say anything back.

Storms

Paul is usually so bright even when we give him a fright
or squirt his shirt or steal his things for our Den. But
today his eyes are cloudy-grey the
water running inside him is churning-wild and stormed.
I still can't believe you threw that kid's bag out the window.
I didn't mean to … It was an accident! And he—
Enough. Paul sighs. *I've got work to do. You can help Joe.*
The young one nods. Blinks. Folds herself small.

This young one

As a general rule we don't like people much. But
sometimes a person comes along who is different.
And we don't know why but something in the darting
of her eyes in the swingswingswinging of her legs the
spinspinspinning of the Rock that she wears at her
neck makes us just a little bit curious. Like
she is the Wind trapped in skin like
she is remembering a song playing inside her too.

Mystery

Paul is still thundering grumbling
stormy-mad and stomping. *I don't understand*,
Paul says, his one human brain straining to
make sense of what his eyes are saying.
Flounder can't just disappear! Where are they going?
We shuffle deep inside our Den so he doesn't see
our skin rippling with tingling bubbles of glee.
It doesn't make sense. And has anyone seen my keys?

School tours

And every day they say the same thing
noses pressed to the glass and they ask
Where is she? Knock knock knock.
Can't you make her come out? Bang bang bang.
What's the point if you can't see her? Tap tap tap.
Is there even an octopus in here? Slap slap slap.
Can we see something else now?
But not today. Today someone asks something different.

A very good question

How did Houdini come to you? Did she walk?
Paul pauses. Eyes staring hard at his young one.
No. She was caught in a fishing net and given to us.
And you aren't part of this tour, so quiet please, Juno.
But, and her voice is tight and burning,
why didn't you put her back?
She was very small and the sea has many dangers. She probably wouldn't have survived. She's safe in here.

Pft.

Like being safe is all
that matters. Like a tank two arms long in
all directions is
any kind of Home. Like
the bubbles from the pump
are enough of an ebb and flow to make us happy
when we know
to be happy is to be free.

Memories

Paul thinks that because we were young when we were
taken that we have forgotten our true Home. Paul thinks
a fake Reef with dead water that's always the same
never changing never waving never washing or
swashing always warm never stormy or cloudy or dim
can fool us into thinking we were never
anywhere else. But
our brains are very good at remembering.

Once

Once, we felt the Rain on our skin the
sink of Sun and shimmer of Moon the
Storm thundering our arms and rumbling from
deep deep inside us.
Once, we danced in the swirl of Tides
curling twirling unfurling and once
we tasted Stars as they fell from the Sky.
Their dust still shines in the night.

Paul's fact

Octopuses are not like humans,
Paul says to the group as he leads them away.
They are not mammals. They do not live in families like us.
Our last common ancestor was a sea worm that lived
550 million years ago! BUT they are super smart.
They can think and remember and use tools and plan.
They like to solve puzzles and play, even though
they have evolved with a totally different kind of mind.

Our fact

People's minds are
not all the same kind
either.
Lots of humans are far
more Octopus than they may think.
We watch Paul's young one from our Den and
wonder at the way her mind ripples like
Waves that wash at the Sand.

Wonderings

And then the young one is at our tank
not slapping
not tapping
not pressing her nose to the glass but
seeing us right here in our Den. Like she can feel our
blood beating
just the way we can feel her.
A Tide pulling us closer.

A strange kind of tug

You're stuck in here too, huh?
Guess he doesn't listen to you either.
He thinks I don't even try.
Maybe I just need to try harder.
She spins the Rock on her neck spinspinspin and
small driplets of Sea leak from her eyes and
ripple down her face. We gentle-drift from our Den
so her words can sink deeper into our skin.

Octospeed

People's singular brains are usually so slow their
bodies so closed to the sounds that are all
the time surrounding them but
not this one. We can feel her brain buzzing her
skin fuzzing with so many thoughts like Lightning her
fingers her feet her thinking too wild to settle and be.
We drift, bloom, pulse and press ourselves to the glass
and say, *We have lots of questions buzzing at our brains too.*

Conversations

The young one stands with her
hand spread wide
on the other side of the glass
and she smiles as if
her skin
can feel our skin
rippling our thoughts and
our feelings too.

And then she comes closer

We did not think this young one would come sneaking come creeping come peeping around behind our tank in the back room where young ones never go. We did not think she would be so curious that her fear of being caught would be fought and squashed down small to deal with later. It seems that she is just as curious as we are.

Introductions

Her eyes are wide and flickering and she is
short-gasp breathing her one human heart
thump pump thwumping so loud it is
footstomps in our brains and she
lifts the lid from our tank
dips her hand deep in the dark cold and whispers,
Hi there. My name is
Juno.

Greetings

And now her hand is in our water flapping and
splashing but gentle and soft as if she is asking
as if she is hoping as if she is
calling our name. We whisper to white and watch
and wait while our nine brains muse and
confuse each other with all of our tumbling wondering.
Okay, we say, and bloom ourselves red puff ourselves
monstrous-wide and swoop and, *Hello. Hello, Juno.*

Nine brains confused

We could pull her into our tank we could drag her
finger by arm by shoulder in and under and
no amount of thundering rage
could make us let her go.
So why do we feel ourselves falling to her calling?
Why do we ridge our skin gather bumps on our arms
and relax ourselves into her hand like there is
a knowing glowing inside her, welcoming us Home?

Taste

All people taste like
outside aquarium but
Juno tastes of
something
more. Juno tastes
like
the
Stars.

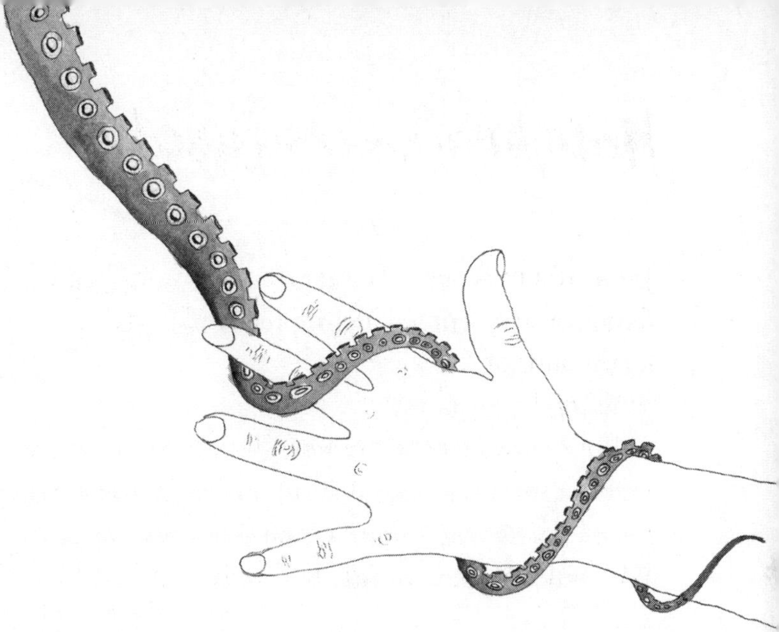

Caught

Juno is so entangled in our arms in
our dance in our
stare that she is not aware
of the shadow
blooming
looming closer
behind her.
Hey! What are you doing back here?

Not yet

Juno tries to wrench her arm
from our grip but we are not ready to
let go and we are
growing larger now
pulling ourselves further now
up her arm up her shoulder up her neck and out and
Oh no you don't, Houdini. Go on now, back you go.
We could argue with Joe, but we don't.

A good observation

Joe! You scared me! I thought you were my dad.
Lucky for you. He wouldn't be happy to find you here.
I know, but … I had to meet her. To … talk to her.
Well, you'd better be careful. She is a regular
escape artist. That's why she's called Houdini.
She is so soft! Not slimy at all! And she seems so wise.
Oh yes. You don't know the half of it.
Do you think she understands what we're saying?

Secret keepers

Joe closes the mesh tight on our tank and says,
It's not night-time, my friend. No exploring. Not yet.
The smile on Juno's face blooms close to bursting.
Does she really go out at night?
Joe puts his finger to his lips. *It's our secret. I know in my head that I should tell, but my heart says no. Sometimes,*
Joe looks at Juno, our marks growing bright on her arm,
hearts are difficult to argue with.

Take a beat

So, Joe says, *your dad said you'll be helping us this week?*
Is that what he said?
Well, he said you are suspended, but here you are helping, so.
Juno shrinks. Juno shuffles. Juno shrivels up tight.
Sometimes I do things before I have time
to think what might happen next.
I'm the same! We just have busy brains full of rowdy thoughts.
I had to train my brain to take a beat. It isn't always easy.

Joe's fact

Before they walk away we hear
Joe say to Juno that we are something of a celebrity.
I have a spot on the radio. I'm always telling Houdini stories,
and we did not know we were famous.
I've learnt a lot working here. Do you know that
octopuses have been around for longer than dinosaurs?
and Juno looks back with eyes grown wide and
What else? she asks. ***What else can you tell me?***

Our fact

We Octopuses do not learn from our mothers
our fathers
our sisters and brothers
our cousins and uncles and aunts but
our memories are
longer than we are and we
hear our Ancestors murmuring always
deep inside our skin.

Waiting

All day long we can hear
that Sea howl prowling wild
inside our brains and every part of us is straining
to feel it taste it twirl it whirl it swirl it
inside our body
again.
Be careful, Spike whispers but
night cannot come fast enough.

The far washroom

Tonight we do not explore or
choose whose tank to visit or
crawl through the door with the boat painted bright or
make our way right to the edge so the
Sea can ripple all through us.
We know there is only one place to go
and we do not know if we can make it but still
we must try.

Losing

Down the long hall
through the door
to the far washroom floor.
That is where we need to be but the
pain is creeping across our skin seeping weeping
burning and pulling and scraping us to
nothing. We shrink shuffle shrivel up tight and wait
for Joe to find us.

Memories

Back in our tank, the singing of the Sea fills our brains
with memories that are meant to be
quiet now. Silent now. Gone now. But
in our sleep we are strong enough to creep to crawl
while all of our nine brains carry us to the drain
down the pipes to
the Sea and in our dreams we
are dancing.

A different morning

We are in the Weeds waiting
when Paul comes in and Juno is right there with him.
Keys jingle-jangling footstomps thundering
flicking the lights at their switch – one, two, three – and
Hey, Houdini! How are you? She smiles
and we shuffle our skin to smooth to red to ripples
of the first Sun sinking in the Sea
and we rise ourselves up to greet her.

Juno's fact

How on Earth? She has never done that before. Paul smiles
then frowns. *You haven't been feeding her, have you?*
I guess she just likes me. I like her too. Joe told me
that octopuses can lift twenty times their own weight.
So she could lift a giant panda! Or a tiger!
But Paul has already turned
forgotten us, moved away.
Is that the time? We're late opening!

Our fact

Giant Pandas and
Tigers do not
live in the Sea or
even in the
aquarium.
But we could lift Paul
if we wanted to. We could
drag him back to Juno.

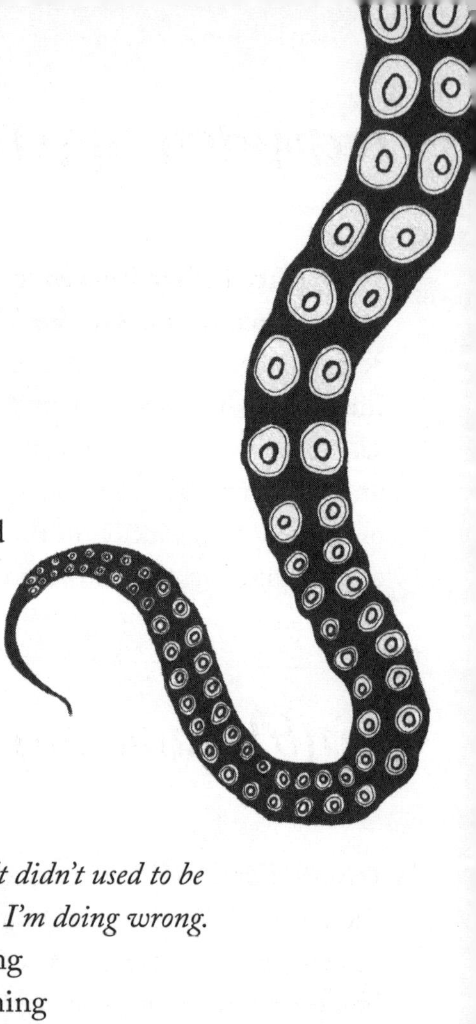

Payback

It's as if I don't even exist. It didn't used to be
like this. I don't know what I'm doing wrong.
Juno is up and down pacing
head-shaking finger-spinning
trying to work Paul out.
We wrap our suckers tight
swell dark green and hope she knows that means
we'll squirt him extra hard next time.

Every day it gets stronger

We want to be like we were before but now we
miss the Sea with every one of our
3,154 suckers.
It is a kind of

ache and our
three hearts feel like they are
break

ing.

Nights turning to days

We try to crush the memory of the singing of the Sea and go back to how we were before. Crossing the floor through the door to the edge, climbing and dining with Flounder and Crabs, nabbing and grabbing Paul's things from his Den to amuse us. Tonight we take a watch. We like the beating of its heart so out of time from ours. But the nights are not full of adventure now that we remember what it is we are missing.

Finders keepers

We do not know what Paul thinks he is doing
with his scooping looping net trying to get at the
treasures in our Den but
this is not a game that he
will be winning.
These treasures are ours now and not for the taking.
Out of the way, Houdini. Let go!
Give me that! The net is not for playing.

No idea

Then Juno is there and she is smiling and
she is laughing at the way we are throwing
Stones at Paul and squirting his shirt
with Dirt and Grit and soaking his face so it is
all over dripping. *Dad, what are you doing?*
My watch! It must have slipped off and now
Houdini won't let me get near it!
Juno takes the net. *Here, let me try.*

Deal

Hey there, Houds. That's some treasure you've got.
We tug at the net so Juno knows we can take it if we want to and she laughs, swirls the net above our head so the water twirls like a whirlpool and makes our skin tingle and fizz.
How about a swap, hey? The watch for a juicy crab?
It is the look of shock on Paul's face that makes us say, ***Okay***. We didn't like that watch much anyway.

Maybe one day

How did you figure that out? Paul asks.
Maybe one day you'll be a keeper too.
Hey, Dad, did you know some aquariums only keep their octopuses for six months, then they release them back into the sea? Maybe we could do that too?
Juno, Houdini is happy here. And a new octopus costs money. Hey! My watch is still working!
And slow and heavy we drift back to our Den.

Discussions

Every night now, I find her all dry on the floor,
Joe tells Juno, and Juno strokes our head
sways her arm in our tank like
we are in the Sea and she
is a Wave carrying us lifting us drifting us closer.
She is trying to get somewhere, but I don't know where.
I'm worried that one night I won't find her in time.
Joe? Do you think she is trying to go … home?

Rain

Sometimes we close our eyes
curl ourselves tight like a Rock and imagine the
thundering of feet rumbling the floor
is the thundering of Clouds of
Rain falling fresh that
the slapping of hands on our glass is the
snapping of fishtails fighting our grip and we imagine
one day we will feel Rain on our skin once again.

Another morning

We are in the Weeds waiting
when Paul and Juno come in all footstomps
whispering voices whispering eyes
searching and quiet.
She hasn't been out of her den for days now,
Juno says and Paul sighs.
Juno, Houdini's getting old. This might be her way of saying goodbye.

A shell

Juno lifts the lid on our tank
dips her hand in the dark cold deep
flapping and splashing but gentle and soft as if
she is asking as if she is hoping as if she is
calling our name. We whisper to white
Okay, we say, but do not bloom ourselves red
puff ourselves monstrous-wide or swoop but
we float. Grey and empty. *Hello. Hello, Juno.*

Aching

What's wrong, Houds?
Houdini? Are you okay?
And Juno holds our arms
strokes our head between our eyes so we
shiver and ripple with moments of bright and
we hold her hand
stroke her face and
hope she understands.

we are not okay.

We cannot tell her of the ache in our hearts that is
shaking us near to breaking while
all we want is to feel the Sea
taste the Sea smell the Sea twist ourselves to Sea
even if it can only be for a single moment more.
We cannot tell her but
we think she'd understand because we
can taste her aching that is shaking her to breaking too.

Planning

Juno sits by the side of our tank
not chittering and chattering not
jiggling or spinning not
smiling or swishing our tank just
scribbling and
scrabbling at the paper in her book
her busy brain flowing in Waves
right onto the page.

An excellent idea

What's that you're drawing? Paul says and Juno turns red
wraps herself in her arms and breathes deep.
It's an idea I had. For a new kind of tank. One that connects
to the sea. That way Houdini could come and go when
she wants and no other creatures could work the
latch or squeeze through. See? It could go over at the
edge of the room – the harbour's right there.
And then she could choose where to be.

Sunshine

Huh. That's really something.
Paul smiles at the book in Juno's hand and
You've got some imagination! I don't think
anyone's thought of a tank like that before.
And Juno blossoms.
Juno swells.
Juno blooms herself tall and bright and
brimming with happy.

Darkness

So, you like it then? Juno says and Paul
gives her shoulder a squeeze and the Tides surging
inside them both beat in time together.
Really! It's great.
So, we'll do it then?
Oh. No. Sorry, kiddo. We can't. We don't have
money for something like this. One day maybe.
But for now we just have to make do.

Lost

Paul's smile fades
and he turns
walks away and
Juno fades
and she turns, tears the page from her book
scrunches it small and lets it fall. All her
happy
sunk deep into the shadows.

Another way?

We watch from our Den as Joe drifts in
moving along to his own silent song and
he sees Juno's plan on the floor. Gentlies it up.
Whispers it open and
Ha! You really know how to think
outside the box, Juno!
Ahhh, Spike says, so slow so wise so sure,
Think outside the box.

How to catch a Fish

Juno, this is really great!
Nah. Forget it. Dad said the aquarium
doesn't have the money.
I was stupid to think we could do it.
What? You're going to give up just like that?
Where's your fight? There's more than one way to catch a fish.
I told you already – Houdini is a celebrity.
I have an idea that might just work …

Planning

Joe is right. What is the use of nine brains if
they are all saying the same thing
the same way every day over and
over again and
maybe we can learn a
thing or two from Joe. There is more than one way
to catch a Fish. It is time to think
outside the tank.

Juno's fact

Hey, Joe, did you know that octopuses can
figure out how other animals think?
What they are scared of or
what they want or
what they won't notice passing by?
That's how octopuses decide what to look like.
It isn't just a reflex.
It's a decision.

Our fact

Paul is a person and people are
Animals too so perhaps all we need to
do is think like a Paul …
What he is scared of and what he wants and
what he won't notice passing by …
We feel an idea surging a
plan emerging and our skin is
tingling wild with maybes.

Last night in the aquarium

We do not use our exit in case the urge
to reach the drain surges
inside us again
and stops us from
thinking. Instead
we plan.
Save our energy.
Tell the Sea we are coming.

True treasure

None of the hoard
we've stored in our Den
is as special as the
treasure Juno gives us on our
very last morning. She drops it in our tank
when no one is looking and
it's as if she knows just what
we are planning.

Spinning Stone

Juno is always
spinspinspinning that
Stone around her neck like
it is holding her
thoughts wrapped together.
It's for you, Houds. I found it at the beach when
I was small. It still smells like the sea.
I thought that maybe you'd like it for your den.

The flavour of memories

We wrap the Juno Stone tight
pass it along every one of our suckers
so we can taste can savour every moment held deep
within its skin
imagining those moments are ours.
And all of our brains burn bright and buzz with the
way it feels in our arms. How it holds Juno inside it so
she can be with us even when she is gone.

If he could speak Octopus

We want Paul to know that when we go we
will miss him. We want Paul to know he made us
almost-happy here with his puzzles and boxes with
snacks deep inside and toys that hide treats to munch on.
We want him to know that we know he
did his best to make us a Home.
But the Sea is a living Beast, too wild to be grown in a
tank and her calling is too strong to resist.

Spike

We tell her *Goodbye*.
We tell her *Good luck*.
We tell her we are going to miss her.
I am remembering, she says
the song that comes
from a thousand seas and I'm
trying to
find the words.

The plan

When the clock dings three times
Paul will try to tidy our tank. We feel the trolley's wheels
rumbling the floor but this time we
are ready.
This time we stretch ourselves
into Paul's mind and put our plan
into action.
Day Octopus style.

Fierce

Houdini! Wow, you've really messed up your tank.
What on Earth have you been doing with the coral?
And the rocks are blocking the pipes again! I'll need the mop.
And that's when we swoop from our Den
with the roar of the Sea
gushing rushing blushing through our skin
turning us to

MONSTER

Disguise

Our skin is all prickles all rickles of black our
back is tracks of rumbling Storms
that swarm our skin that cloud our skin and
shroud us in patches of wild-fierce rememberings.
We fill our gills close to bursting squirt a
spurt of water so furious so strong at the
light that it fizz-sparks and spits to dark
wrapping us tight. Holding us close.

Invisible

While Paul is trying to find his torch to
light his way to steady the
spray that's flooding the floor
we pour from our tank
eight arms nine brains three hearts and 3,154 suckers
twist ourselves to mop to cloth to sponge
wet and crumpled
in the very bottom of the bucket.

Hope

We hear Paul call for Juno to
help clean up all of our mess and
Where is she, Dad? I can't see her anywhere.
She must be back in her den. What has got into her?
And we wait while the cloths and sponges
fall around us keeping us wet keeping us
hoping that maybe our plan is
working.

The final goodbye

Gah! I'll call the electrician. Juno, do what you can
then take this lot back to the washroom, will you?
We'll have to sort out the mess in Houdini's tank later.
From the bottom of the bucket we
hear Paul's footstomps thundering
his keys jingle-jangling
for the very
last time.

Thanks for all the treasure

We tell Paul, *Goodbye Good morning Goodnight*
and think of the keys
phone
headphone
Swiss Army knife
pen
paperweight and all the other
treasures we left behind for him to find in our Den.

So close

Juno whistles while she wheels us
down the long long hall
with the walls of Fish
right through the door
to the far washroom floor and
we hear the whisper of Wind of
Rain and of midnight Moons
edging closer.

Busy-brained

And then Juno stops and
the mop in her hand clashes to the
floor and our hearts are crashing right with
it. She must have seen us must have
been too busy-brained to be fooled.
Juno! Wait! I've got something to tell you!
Joe, did you see what Houdini did to her tank?
I did! I guess she heard the good news about your plan …

Brimming

We can taste Juno's joy like Waves
that crash from her skin into the air and rain down
in drips all around us. And she is buzzing she
is bustling she is all over tingling with excitement.
Wait – what? Your idea worked? For real?
I told you Houdini was famous! As soon as I shared your
plan on the radio, the donations started flooding in.
Everyone wants to help – come on, I'll show you.

A different ache

Juno leaves us in the washroom
not knowing we are there
not knowing we are going and
will not be seeing her
again. We hold tight to our Juno Stone
and pretend it is
Juno we are
holding.

Waiting

We must be patient.
We must be careful.
We must make sure there is
no one near enough to see us here to
watch us slide and glide and slip and
dip our way from the bucket to the trolley
to the floor to the drain just
waiting to carry us Home.

Now

It is quiet now
empty now
all the voices are far now
our skin is feeling itchy now
and the Sea she is
calling now.
It is time now.
Time to go Home now.

Ecstasy

And so we go.
We pour from the bucket to the
cool of the floor and we
soar
to the drain with
every one of our
nine brains
thrilling.

Footstomps

But now – and we freeze, turn ourselves to
Stone to brick to wall to Rock to sponge to cloth –
footstomps are thundering blundering sundering
voices are clammering yammering hammering
blabbering babbling and we are so so close –
Where could she be? Check the washrooms!
                              and yet so so
very far.

Juno

Juno sees us here on the floor
by the wide-open drain
and her one human brain puts
all the pieces together. Octospeed.
The sea! You <u>are</u> trying to get back home!
Her smile ripples her cheeks lighting her up from the
inside but then
Juno pauses.

Silenced

Juno stops.
Her rippling light turns to white to grey to empty shell
and we can see she
is training her brain to
slow. To take a beat. To
think what might happen before she acts.
Dad told me to find you. He says we can't afford to lose you.
And we're going to make you a new tank, and—

Hopeless

And
we
know
what
is
going
to
happen.

Listening

Juno reaches her arms towards us
the Sea inside her churning
her heart yearning and we watch Juno shrink.
Juno shuffle. Juno shrivel up tight.
Do you remember what Joe said? In his head he knows what to do but his heart says no. Sometimes –
and we watch Juno grow. Juno bloom. Juno blossom –
hearts are difficult to argue with.

Goodbye

She's not here! Juno calls and, *Go!* she whispers
and the taste of her arm wrapped tight in ours
is the taste of
Seas that are wild and
Winds that are fierce and a Sun that burns
hot bright and furious in the Sky. It is a
knowing that we will carry her Sea deep inside us
always.

Drain

And then we are
in the drain and we are sliding
through the pipes gliding through the
walls while all around us the
calling of the Sea is louder and stronger and
wilder and fiercer than ever before.
Welcoming us
back Home.

This.

We are Home. Back Home with the
Sea flowing around us
growing us blooming us strong and *this*
the pull the push the tumble of Tides the
rumble of Storms soon approaching *this*
is why we decided to go. Because no
matter how hard Paul tried *this*
can never be faked.

Song of a thousand Seas

Our skin is alive now is rippling is swirling is
twirling with the singing of the Sea
a Beast more WILD than we are
and she tastes of infinite mornings and
blossoming nights and tells tales with every ebb every
flow those billions of years of knowings in each drop.
Now we are part of that song once again …

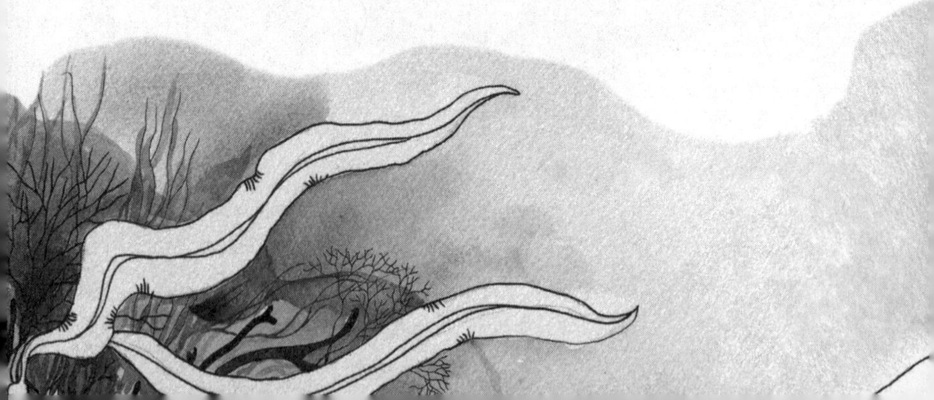

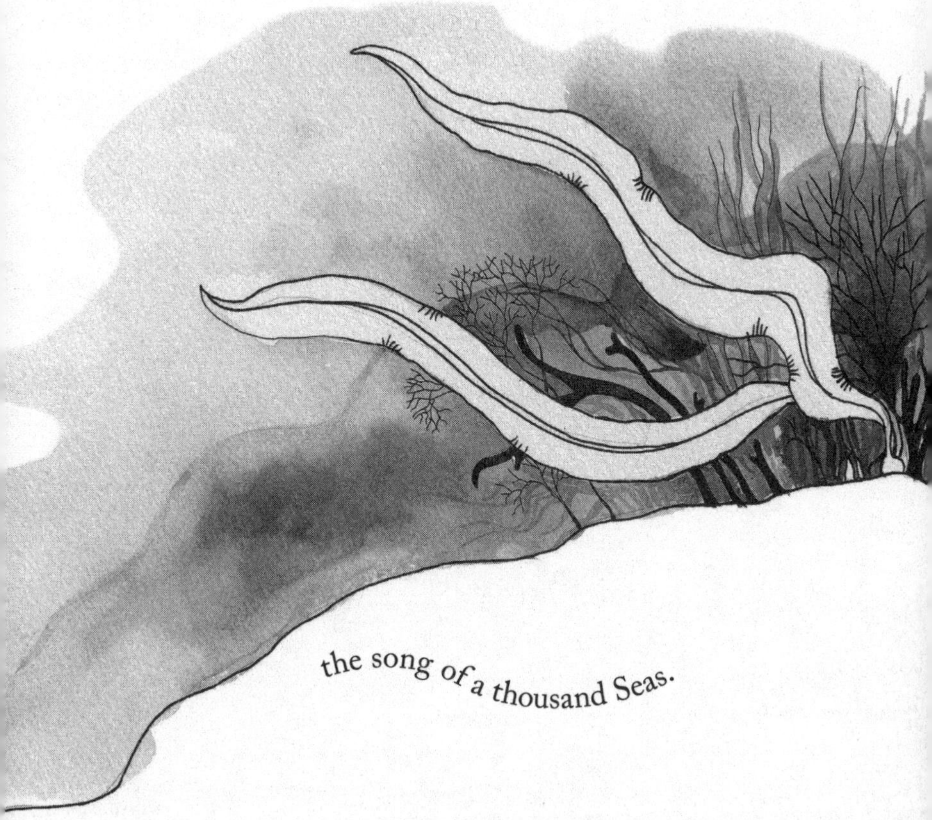

the song of a thousand Seas.

BRAND NEW EXHIBIT!

Welcome to the reef!

Is there anyone lurking in this tank? Maybe!

This tank is a WORLD FIRST. It allows our resident octopus to come and go as she pleases. Our keepers train the octopus so she knows that she will always find food and safety here when she wants it. No other sea creatures can work the locks and the latches, nor squeeze themselves through the holes to get into the tank.

Octopuses are very good at figuring out solutions to problems and like to keep their nine brains busy. A tank like this only works because octopuses are very, very smart.

Can you think like an octopus?

Juno's octopus facts

1. There are so many different types of octopuses! There are about 300 species that we know of, and new species are still being discovered. From the giant Pacific octopus, which weighs up to 272 kilograms and stretches over 9 metres long, to the tiny Wolfi octopus, which weighs less than a gram and is only 1 centimetre long. Some octopuses glow in the dark, some have fins that look like ears, and some, like the glass octopus, are see-through.

2. Octopuses have beaks! If you want to know whether an octopus can squeeze through an opening, measure their beak – anything their beak can fit through, the octopus can fit through. And octopus beaks have venom. Most octopus venom isn't dangerous to humans, but it can paralyse other animals.

3. The blue-ringed octopus is one of the most venomous animals in the world. They only grow to about 10 centimetres long, but they have enough venom to kill twenty-six fully grown humans! Blue-ringed octopuses are not aggressive, though, and they are only known to bite people when they feel threatened.

4. Octopuses are playful, curious and incredibly smart. They can solve problems, find their way through a maze, predict what might happen to them, use tools and plan ahead. They are also very observant, recognising people's faces as well as remembering which routes from their den are dangerous. They are known to carry shells to hide under when travelling from their den, and to use the poisonous tentacles of some jellyfish to defend against predators! They also have excellent memories and can learn by watching other octopuses and other animals. This means that they learn which animals are dangerous or poisonous and can imitate more dangerous animals to scare predators away.

5. Octopuses have been living in the oceans for more than 330 million years. That's more than ten times as long as *Homo sapiens* have been on Earth and long before dinosaurs existed.

6. Octopuses can regrow arms! When an arm is bitten off by a predator, it continues to move, luring the predator away. But scientists have found that octopuses can also recognise their own amputated arms, and they will even carry them back to their den.

7. Octopuses have nine brains. They have one brain in each arm and a central brain in their head. This

means that each arm can perform different tasks. Each arm has hundreds of suckers, and these suckers can feel, taste and smell. They can also work like a finger and thumb to pick things up.

8. Octopuses live throughout the oceans and seas, from the deep sea to shallow reefs. They make their dens in all sorts of things – reefs, shells, glass bottles, gumboots, jars, burrows in mud and holes in rocks. They also collect materials to make their dens better, and clean the things they collect. Although octopuses mostly live alone, some octopuses, like the gloomy octopus, have also been found to live in 'octopus villages' like Octopolis and Octlantis in New South Wales, Australia, where the octopuses have built their dens close together.

9. Octopuses are remarkable creatures, but they don't live for very long. While an octopus can lay thousands of eggs, only 1 per cent of the octopus babies (or larvae) are likely to survive until adulthood. Those who do survive usually only live for a few years. Male octopuses often die shortly after mating. For most species of octopus, the female octopus will die just before, or shortly after, her eggs hatch.

10. Octopus mothers are incredible carers! They may not be able to look after their babies once they hatch,

but they do everything they can to protect them while they can. After the female octopus has laid her eggs, she stays in her den, guarding and tending to her eggs until they hatch. Octopus mothers clean the eggs and regulate the temperature of the water by using their arms and siphons to keep the water clean, cool and moving. During this time, the octopus mother will not leave her den – not even to hunt for food! She will go months or even years without food so she can protect her eggs until they are ready to hatch.

11. Octopuses have blue blood. This is because they have more copper in their blood than humans, which helps oxygen spread through their body in very low temperatures.

12. Octopuses have three hearts. Two hearts pump the blood through their gills and one circulates the blood to the organs. The heart that circulates the blood stops beating while swimming, though. This is why octopuses prefer to crawl along the sea floor rather than swim – it is far less exhausting.

13. Many octopuses have ink sacs, which means they can squirt ink when they are in danger. Ink is made from melanin (the same dark pigment that is in a person's hair and skin). The ink also contains tyrosinase, which

burns the eyes of a predator and can temporarily stop the predator from tasting and smelling.

14. Octopuses have webbing between their arms made from skin. They can throw this over their prey like a blanket to stop the prey from escaping.

Author's note

Ideas for books come from all sorts of odd places. This one came to me in a dream. In the dream, I was an octopus. I saw through octopus eyes and felt my way with octopus arms. I tasted with my skin and swam towards the gentle light filtering through the water from the sun. This dream was unlike any dream I had had before and unlike any I have had since. The very next morning I sent a message to my publisher and told her this was the book I had to write. I wish I could have that dream again. I wish I could be an octopus again. This book is my attempt to get as close to that dream as possible, both for myself and for you readers.

In trying to understand the world from the point of view of an octopus, I had to do a lot of research. I knew very little about octopuses before that dream and had a lot to learn. Entering the world of the octopus has been a wonderful, eye-opening journey. I have discovered how very little we humans know about the sea and her myriad life forms, and how magical and breathtaking the facts that we do know are. I have learnt how deeply we humans impact the sea and how far reaching those impacts are. I have been awestruck time and time again by recounts and videos of octopus encounters and escapades – each one confirming just how remarkable and intelligent octopuses are. This story is based loosely on one of the most famous escapes of all – the escape of Inky from the National Aquarium of New Zealand. In fact, all of Houdini's antics in this book are based on real-life octopus hijinks. But best of all, my research gave me the opportunity to meet and fall in love with an octopus.

After contacting SEA LIFE Sydney Aquarium, I was invited to meet the real Houdini and her amazing keeper, Chelsea. Chelsea showed me all the workings of the aquarium, took me to the food preparation areas, showed me where they keep Houdini's toys and told me all about what it is like to care for octopuses. And then I was taken to meet Houdini. Nothing could have prepared me for the experience.

Houdini was cheeky and curious and so, so smart. She distracted me with six of her arms while simultaneously sneaking up behind me to startle me with her other two arms. She tried multiple times to crawl from her tank and seemed as keen to get to know me as I was to get to know her. The most wonderful moment came when I rubbed the spot between her eyes, the way I do with my dogs at home. I hadn't meant to do it. I was transfixed and it was almost as if we were having a conversation. As soon as I began rubbing, Houdini stilled. She had been a bundle of activity before then, but in that moment, it felt as though she was listening. She then reached around to hold my arm as if in reply.

Houdini died a few months after my visit, but her voice remained very firmly in my head throughout the writing of this book. Being an author is always an imperfect act of translation. I hope I have done Houdini's incredible mind justice.

The print you see here is Houdini's sucker print – her signature. For this book is as much hers as it is mine.

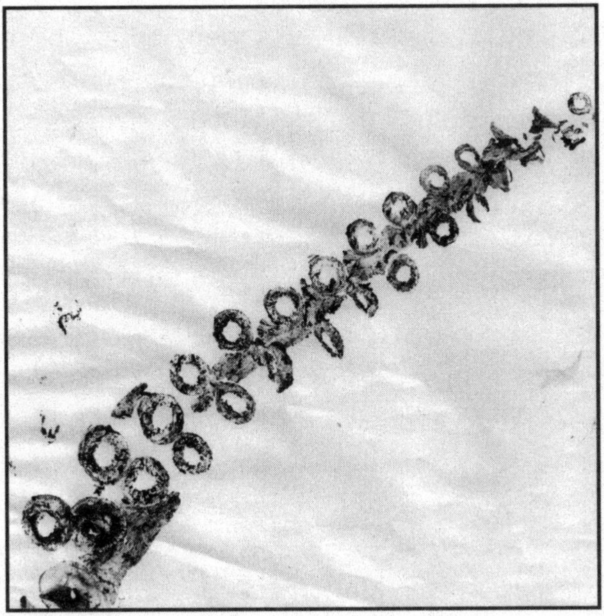

Acknowledgements

This book has been a long time coming. It has shapeshifted many times, exploring many skins along the way. There are always many people to thank when bringing a book to life, but this one feels like it had help from more people than most.

Thanks first and foremost to the amazing team at UQP, and to Cathy Vallance, whose incredible flexibility, resolute support and expert guidance enthusiastically enabled me to find a way to write this story despite my ongoing health struggles. A huge thank you also to my wonderful editor, Felicity Dunning, who made the process so brilliantly smooth and easy. Working with you on this has been nothing short of delightful. I hope it is the first book of many we can work on together.

To the incredible Aviva Reed, who so beautifully brought Houdini to life on the page. Only someone who can think outside of themselves can bring such a distinct sense of the more-than-human world to life in this way. I remain your biggest fan.

To Clair Hume, who listened to my octopus dream with delight. Clair's enthusiasm and support for this story, in all its varied forms, never wavered and I am delighted to finally have found a way to let this story find its readers.

Many thanks, as always, to my brilliant agent, Claire

Wilson, and the team at RCW – I know we joked about me becoming the overly obsessed octopus lady, well, here we are … Thank you for your constant encouragement and assurances and for always seeing the spark.

This book couldn't have been written without the willingness of SEA LIFE Sydney Aquarium to not only answer all my questions, but to invite me behind the scenes to see how it all worked. Huge thanks to Denice Askebrink and Benjamin Buchanan for indulging me. The enthusiasm, care, attention and genuine love for the aquarium creatures was evident from the moment I walked in. I will be forever grateful especially to Chelsea Rowe – Houdini's keeper and friend. Chelsea is a fount of knowledge and an incredibly compassionate and dedicated keeper. The love shared between Houdini and Chelsea was obvious, and their friendship lies at the heart of this story. Thank you, Chelsea, for everything – the photos, the videos, and for Houdini.

I would also like to thank the octopus community of experts and fans, who helped shape my knowledge, and to my writing community – large and small – who keep me going and keep me inspired through it all. Huge thanks especially to Penny Harrison, Penni Russon, Kate Mildenhall, Cath Moore, Simmone Howell and Bec Kavanagh for being my people.

Finally, and always, to my incredible family, who encourage my obsessions and make this all possible: Mischa, Mina, Luca and Jugs, you are everything.

Zana Fraillon (she/they) is an internationally acclaimed, multi-award-winning author of books for children and young adults. Her work has been published in over fifteen countries and is in development for both stage and screen. She has a doctorate in creative writing, and degrees in history and teaching. Zana's passion for empowering young people to find their voice is a feature of both her books and her work with writers of all ages.

Also by Zana Fraillon
THE WAY OF DOG

Be strong. Be fierce. Life is more than a concrete floor.

Scruffity is born into the harsh, grey world of a puppy farm. Taken from his mamma and locked in a concrete cage, what he yearns for most is Family. To belong is The Way of Dog. But no one wants him.

Just as his chances of adoption grow dangerously thin, Scruffity is set free by a boy as unwanted and lonely as he is. Outside, Scruffity learns all about The Way of Dog – it is to run, to dig, to howl and, biggest of all, to love. But when tragedy strikes, Scruffity is suddenly all alone.

How does a dog find his way home when he never had one to begin with?

> 'This book has a timeless quality that feels like the work of Kate DiCamillo. It's a book that is heartbreaking yet equally heartwarming.' ***Readings***

ISBN 978 0 7022 6556 3

Turn the page for a peek inside *The Way of Dog* …

UQP

THE WAY OF DOG

Dear Shoe-Legs
Are you coming? Are you? Are you?
Then shake wide awake and take my advice
throw the Burs from your fur and
sliiiiiiide on the Ice.
Come flat-foot follow and paw-pad my way
for I have a thing
or four
to say about living this life according to
The Way of Dog.

And if you're coming prick your ears
pause your paws and
listen sharp
stretch your limbs
swell your lungs with every howl
every scrowl with a full-blown

RRRRRRRROOOOOOWWWWWWWWLLLLL

for this story is LOUD
it's made to be growled
to be bellowed and roared to be
freed from your jaws to
travel Wind-wide and find those ears and
souls all waiting.

So come scramper
come trample
come schnuffle about
come discover this world
from a Dog's point of snout.
Are you coming? Are you? Are you?

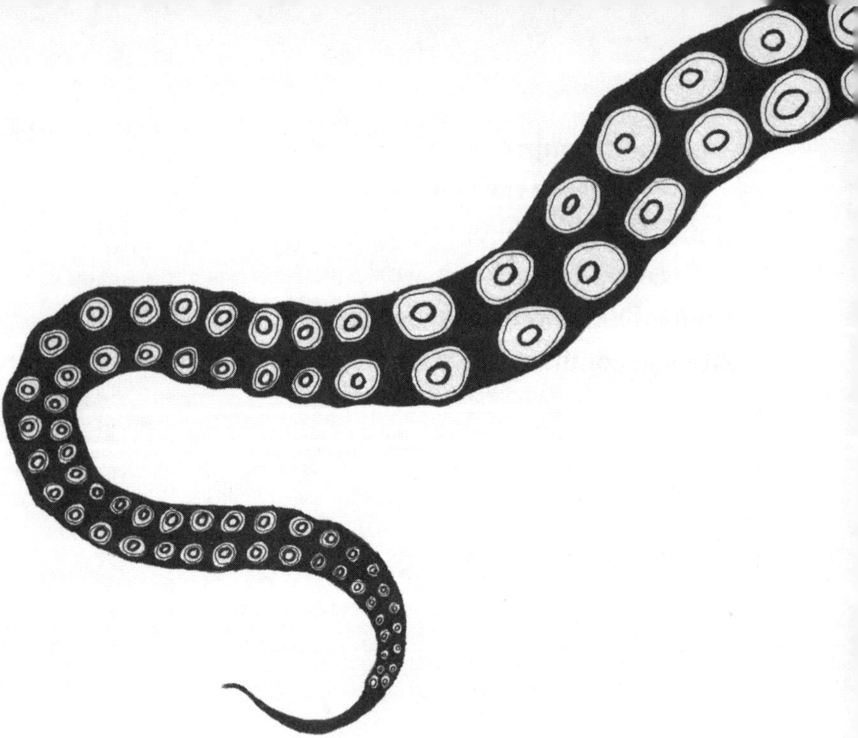

FOOTBALL LEGENDS

KYLIAN MBAPPE

ED HAWKINS

FOOTBALL LEGENDS

KYLIAN MBAPPE

SCHOLASTIC

Scholastic Australia
PO Box 579 Gosford NSW 2250
ABN 11 000 614 577
www.scholastic.com.au

Part of the Scholastic Group
Sydney • Auckland • New York • Toronto • London • Mexico City
New Delhi • Hong Kong • Buenos Aires • Puerto Rico

First published in the UK by Scholastic Ltd in 2021.
This edition published by Scholastic Australia in 2024.

While this book is based on real characters and actual historical events, some situations and people are fictional, created by the author.

UNAUTHORIZED: this book is not sponsored, approved or endorsed by any person who appears in this book.

ISBN 978-1-761-52741-8

Printed in China by Hang Tai Printing Company Limited.

MIX
Paper | Supporting responsible forestry
FSC® C023121
FSC www.fsc.org

10 9 8 7 6 5 4 3 2 1 24 25 26 27 28 / 2

Contents

THE BOY FROM BONDY

In Bondy, a northern and poor suburb of Paris, France, there are three murals which help to guide and inspire people through everyday life. They are of Kylian Mbappé, one of their own. The boy from Bondy who played on their streets and became the greatest footballer in the world.

The first is a picture of a young Kylian fast asleep in the green strip of local club AS Bondy, dreaming about wearing France's number 10 shirt. The second shows him wearing the kit of Paris Saint-Germain. "Bondy Ville des Possibles" ("Bondy, City of Possibilities") is the slogan.

Finally, the third has Kylian smiling in front of a French flag. It reads, "'98 was a great year for French football. Kylian was born."

In 1998, of course, France won their first World Cup. Kylian would be the nineteen-year-old superstar who would propel them to their second title.

Kylian is not just the face of Bondy – or that of Paris Saint-Germain, the European superclub who are aiming to take down giants like Real Madrid and Barcelona for Champions League domination – but of French football. It's not Paul Pogba. Or Antoine Griezmann. Kylian is more famous than the two of them combined.

He is known the world over for his blistering pace and brilliant finishing. For the records that he smashes. And for the list of trophies and titles that most footballers could only dream of. But Kylian is not finished yet.

He has a plan to win everything, everywhere. A plan which he decided upon at a very young age.

It is why when he was standing in the tunnel before France's World Cup final victory over Croatia in Moscow in 2018 that he felt perfectly relaxed and ready to enjoy the biggest game of his life. It is why it felt like he was having a kickabout with friends when he destroyed Argentina and Lionel Messi in the knockout stages.

Kylian was born for these moments.

This is a story about how he made them.

READY FOR STARDOM

Kylian Mbappé Lottin was born on 20 December 1998. The apartment he lived in with his mum and dad overlooked the football stadium of the local team, AS Bondy. His father, Wilfried, was a football coach there, his mother, Fayza, was a former professional handball player and his adopted brother, Jirès, was in the youth team. Oh, and there was also cheeky younger brother Ethan, whom Kylian would play *FIFA* with all day if he had the chance!

It seemed inevitable to Wilfried and Fayza that Kylian would be interested in the beautiful game, but even they were surprised by the single-minded determination and obsession he showed from an early age. As soon as Kylian could talk, he was not shy in telling anyone who would listen (and those who wouldn't) that he was going to be one of the best players in the world.

Wilfried even has a recording of Kylian, at about the age of four or five, telling his dad exactly what he would achieve in the game. When he was six years old he would practise being interviewed by football reporters after a match-winning performance. He would answer the questions about the brilliant goals he had scored or the amazing solo runs to set up others. So Kylian's talent extended beyond football to predicting the future.

Cristiano Ronaldo, the Real Madrid star, was his hero. Kylian's bedroom wall was covered with posters of the Portuguese player. When he was playing football he would try to mimic Cristiano and told his friends he was going to be just like him. He also had posters of Zinedine Zidane, the legendary French World Cup-winning captain on his bedroom wall and, amazingly, Neymar, the Brazilian superstar who would one day become his Paris Saint-Germain teammate. Today,

Neymar finds this funny and refuses to believe it is a true story.

And if he wasn't playing football, Kylian was watching football. His dad remembers him sitting in front of the television for hour after hour. Sometimes he would watch four matches in a row if possible.

The only time Kylian didn't seem to have his mind solely on football was when his mum and dad bought him a toy 4x4 truck at the age of three. He was able to sit in the truck and pedal it around, pretending it was the real thing. They let him pedal down the street and across the road to football training. He was obsessed with it. But little did his parents know that Kylian was just imagining that he was a footballer driving an expensive car to training. Now he jokes "all that was missing was my bag of toiletries". Of course, when he got to training he didn't give the truck a second glance. All he wanted was the football, to run, dribble and shoot for goal.

The Dreamer

Despite thinking about football all the time, Kylian still had to go to school. So what sort of student was he?

He was a daydreamer, often being told off by his teachers for not concentrating. Instead he was thinking about scoring goals or fancy tricks. He didn't like to be sat in a stuffy classroom. Kylian had too much energy! He wanted to be on the move, running, playing and kicking a ball.

His mum and dad thought – and his teachers now agree – that because Kylian was so convinced that he was going to be a professional footballer he reckoned school was just not for him. At the age of five, his mum was so worried about his schoolwork that she sent her son to a psychologist to check if he had difficulty learning. There was no problem. Kylian was very clever. Perhaps too clever sometimes.

When he was set an intelligence test at school, he passed with flying colours with one of the highest marks in the class. The problem was there was a second part to the test and when Kylian was told he had to take the exam instead of playing outside, he messed it up on purpose.

Kylian was cheeky, his teachers remember. When he was six, after he was told off in class, one teacher punished Kylian by telling him to "go into the playground and pick up ten pieces of rubbish". Kylian went outside, tore up a sheet of paper into ten pieces and came straight back. His teacher saw him do it. "Find me ten more."

At the age of ten, Kylian was sent to a Catholic school because his parents were still worried that he was not doing well enough at school. He had a report card which was given to children who misbehaved. At the end of each lesson the teacher would write down whether he had been bad or good. There were not very many good remarks. The teachers complained that he would answer back to them or tease them.

It was unusual for Kylian to tease his classmates, though. The one time he did do that, making fun of a boy for wearing a jumper, his mother taught him a lesson. The next day, she made him wear silly clothes – flared trousers and trainers with Velcro straps. His mum was teaching him to respect others.

Despite his parents' confidence in his ability they

told him it was important to have a good education in case football didn't work out. Kylian also had tennis lessons, sang in a choir and learned to play the flute.

There is little doubt that Kylian could not have made it as one of the top players in the world without a calm upbringing by his mum and dad. Fayza was desperate to make sure that her son grew up to be hard-working and grateful, not spoilt or arrogant. When Kylian was playing for Monaco she found out that somebody else was cleaning his football boots. She was furious. "I forbid you from having someone else clean your boots," she told him. "You come from Bondy with strong human values. Don't start getting into habits like that."

'Beep Beep'

Fayza and Wilfried met in the late 1980s at a youth club in Bondy. Wilfried then set up a new youth club, called Le Petit Bar. This was the start of a football revolution in Bondy which would produce many professional players. Wilfried would organise Saturday kickabouts, and soon they had so many kids wanting to play that they started their own league.

It was so successful that AS Bondy, the local club, realised they needed to be involved. They asked Wilfried to come and coach their youth teams. And soon the kids followed. AS Bondy now has almost 1,000 members and multiple kids' teams, including three girls' teams.

Wilfried, Kylian's dad, was a serious man who spoke with a deep voice. Everyone who met him respected him. Without Wilfried, there probably wouldn't have been the huge interest in playing football in Bondy. He had a huge influence on a number of players and Kylian was not the only one he helped to achieve stardom.

From the age of two, Kylian would go to watch and listen to his dad coach. He would kick a ball in the club's corridors and sit in on team meetings. He was so good as a young player for Bondy that he would play in the age groups two years ahead. He was nicknamed 'Beep Beep' after the character Road Runner from the *Looney Tunes* cartoons because he was so fast.

Coach of Stars

Wilfried, Kylian's dad, has not been just a huge influence on his son's career. He has helped launch the professional career of other players thanks to his coaching at AS Bondy.

For a start, there are two France internationals. Jonathan Ikoné, who plays for Lille, and Sébastien Corchia, who has played in Spain for Sevilla and Espanyol, were both coached by Wilfried at Bondy. Other players he coached at the club include ...

William Saliba: signed for Arsenal for £27 million in 2019
Joé Kobo: midfielder who played for Lille's B team
Metehan Güçlü: young striker who has played for Paris Saint-Germain and Rennes

Fabrice N'Sakala: left-back who has starred for Troyes, Anderlecht and Alanyaspor
Mourad Satli: defender who has played in Belgium, Romania and Qatar
Steeven Joseph-Monrose: winger who has had a successful career in France and Belgium
Ben Sangaré: attacking midfielder who has played in France's second league, Ligue 2

One of the most important footballing lessons Kylian received was from his mum. He was eleven years old and was playing in the semi-final of a local tournament. He described this match as a turning point in his life.

It was played in a real football stadium in Gagny, in the eastern suburb of Paris. Kylian had never played in a proper stadium before, nor had he ever seen so many spectators. It was the first, and only, time in his life that confidence seemed to drain out of him. He could barely kick the ball, let alone run.

Kylian can even remember the day of the week the match was played. It was a Wednesday. He says, "I was terrified. I mean, really, I practically didn't run I was so scared. I barely touched the ball. And I will never forget, after the match, my mother walked out onto the pitch and grabbed me by the ears."

She told him, "You are going to remember this all your life. You always have to believe in yourself, even if you fail. You can miss sixty goals. No one cares. But the fact that you refuse to play because you're scared, it can haunt you all your life."

Those words changed Kylian to the point that he was never scared on a football pitch again. It is why, when he had a trial at Chelsea soon after that experience, he was excited. It was why he was excited standing in the tunnel before the World Cup final in Russia. Before the biggest game of life. He was excited before his first ever professional game for Monaco at the age of sixteen. He knew he was ready and able to show everybody how good he was. No fear.

2

ACADEMY STAR

In September 2011, at the age of twelve, Kylian swapped the hustle and bustle of city life for the peace and quiet of the forest. He swapped the comfort of home life with his family for a small room with boys he didn't know. He swapped Bondy for Clairefontaine, the world-famous French football academy which has produced some of the country's greatest stars.

Kylian was still getting into trouble at his school and his parents felt that he would be better suited to an education which was tailored around football. The family knew Clairefontaine well – his brother Jirès had attended.

For most boys it wasn't an easy decision to go to such a brilliant academy. In fact, it was not a decision at all. You had to be selected. Clairefontaine takes only twenty-three new boys every year. They pick the best of the best from in and around Paris. Thierry Henry, Nicolas Anelka, Louis Saha and William Gallas are all former students.

It is such an elite academy that a player has to be exceptional to be selected. Would you believe that Anthony Martial, the Manchester United star, and N'Golo Kanté, Premier League title winner and World Cup winner, were not deemed good enough?

Once there the boys are left in no doubt about how lucky they are. It is the first step on the ladder to becoming not just a professional footballer, but one of the best in France. Even the French national team train there for matches. It is state of the art, with five-star hotels, libraries, cinemas, seven grass pitches, three synthetic pitches, fitness centres and restaurants.

In the hallways there are pictures of all the famous graduates. One of them is Kylian. His face seems to be on every wall. He wrote on one picture, "Thank you for two wonderful years." There is even a special area dedicated to all the newspaper reports and headlines about Kylian.

Coaches and teachers work so hard to improve the boys' footballing ability. They focus on their technique, improving decision-making and timing how quickly they can turn with a ball and without. They take intelligence tests and are set puzzles to solve. Clairefontaine was the first academy in the world to be so detailed and obsessive about training young players.

Although it is difficult to be selected, there was never any doubt that Kylian would be able to go. As soon as the coaches at Clairefontaine saw him play, they desperately wanted him. They recognised that he was freakishly good for his age.

Instead, it was down to Kylian to select Clairefontaine. After the success of Clairefontaine, many clubs in France had copied the programme and set up their own academies, and Kylian had been very close to joining the French Ligue 1 team RC Lens as part of their youth programme that had developed players like Raphaël Varane and Serge Aurier.

So what happened? Just before Kylian was going to join them, Lens were relegated from the top division.

So Kylian decided it wasn't as good, and chose Clairefontaine.

Slow Start

Thierry Henry is the player that Kylian has been most compared to throughout his career because of their similar style of play. But at Clairefontaine they were compared for a different reason: they didn't impress the coaches immediately. Thierry struggled to fit in with the players and was criticised for not working hard enough. Kylian's problem was that he could sulk if things did not go his way. So much so that he had a nickname – Mbebe (pronounced M-baby).

Why was Kylian so frustrated? Well, it was because he was so desperate to do well and be the best player. But he wasn't the best player and that used to make him angry. That was Arnaud Nordin, a striker who would score loads of goals, often supplied by Kylian who was on the wing. Arnaud now plays in the top French division, Ligue 1, for Saint-Étienne.

Still, Arnaud and Kylian were friends. Arnaud

knew that Kylian was being fiercely competitive and wanted to win and be the best at everything. Arnaud also said that Kylian was great fun and if they were playing in a match and he dribbled past him he would turn round and say, "Did you see how I did that?"

Life at Clairefontaine

- Players attend from Sunday to Friday
- They play for their local clubs on Saturday
- All Clairefontaine teams train in the 4-3-3 formation
- Lessons start at 8 am and finish at 3 pm
- They train for two hours from 4.30 pm
- There is homework in the evenings. But if it's a Champions League night first-year students can watch the first half and second-year students the whole match
- If a boy is late for training he is made to run for the number of minutes he is late by. Ten minutes late, ten minutes running.

Away from the pitch, Kylian was really popular. He would play football in the corridors or *FIFA* on his computer with his first-year room-mate Armand Laurienté, who now plays as a striker for FC Lorient. Armand would be Barcelona and Kylian would be Real Madrid so he could be his idol, Cristiano Ronaldo.

At Clairefontaine, Kylian learned to be patient with his body. He wasn't the best because he wasn't as strong as some of the other players, like Arnaud, who had developed faster physically. He adapted his game. The head coach at Clairefontaine, Jean-Claude Lafargue, said that he stayed clear of defenders and made sure his first touch of the ball was made with extra movement to take them by surprise.

From Sunday to Friday, Kylian worked hard at Clairefontaine. He even played football when he was supposed to be asleep. When all the lights were out, Kylian would sneak out of bed, put on his training shoes and go outside with a ball, shining a torch to find his way. He would practise all his skills and try to recreate the latest wonder goal by Cristiano Ronaldo, all the time 'commentating' to himself about what he was doing. And once the ball hit the net, he would practise his goal celebration too!

On a Saturday he would play again for Bondy, coached by his father. And his dad made sure he kept his feet on the ground. Kylian remembers one game he was playing for Bondy when he heard the voice of his Clairefontaine coach in his head: "Work on your weaker foot!" So when Kylian received the ball on the wing, he worked the ball to his left foot. He tried a long pass with his left and lost the ball. The other team counter-attacked and almost scored. His dad was really angry.

"Kylian! You are not here to try your fancy Clairefontaine experiences! We have a league to play here! You can go back to Clairefontaine all week and train on your nice field! But this is Bondy! Here, we also have a life!"

That was an important lesson for Kylian. He was a player in a team. And for that team, winning was everything.

By his second year at Clairefontaine, Kylian had grown bigger and stronger. He would count all the goals and assists he made in training. The coaches said his game had 'exploded' in his last six months.

He could play with his back to goal, use both his left and right foot, was much better at tracking back, made clever runs off the ball and was faster than ever before. Also his finishing was excellent.

Everyone could see how good he was going to be. One coach said he thought he'd be a future winner of the Ballon d'Or, the yearly award given to the best player in the world.

3

FOOTBALL LEGENDS

THE REAL DEAL

For his tenth birthday, a family friend of the Mbappés gave Kylian a model of the Santiago Bernabéu Stadium, the home ground of Real Madrid. They joked that one day they would buy tickets for a match. Kylian was not fazed. He responded by saying that he would get them seats in the directors' box – because he would be playing for the famous Spanish club.

Four years later, Kylian's confidence proved right. Real Madrid wanted him to go for a trial. Scouts had been watching Kylian at Bondy and they were wowed by his brilliant play. They had also been closely following his work at Clairefontaine. Kylian could hardly believe it. Cristiano Ronaldo, his hero, played for Real.

Real were desperate for Kylian to sign for them and they worked hard to impress the youngster and his family. For a start, Zinedine Zidane, another of Kylian's idols, showed him round the training complex. It was difficult for Kylian to take it all in and he had to pinch himself to check it was really happening.

It was the week of Kylian's fourteenth birthday, and this meant the Mbappés regarded it as a holiday and a treat for their son. Wilfried, Fayza and Kylian's brother Ethan all travelled too. His dad said: "We did not go to Madrid to learn more about our son's potential but to please him."

Would you believe that Zidane also picked Kylian up at the airport in a flashy car? Kylian froze and asked: "Should I take my shoes off?"

"Of course not," laughed Zizou, "get in."

Kylian was still in a daze as they drove to the training ground. "I was just thinking to myself, I am in Zizou's car," he said. "I am Kylian from Bondy. This is not real. I must still be sleeping on the airplane."

And guess what? Kylian even met Ronaldo!

The superstar put his arm round Kylian and gave a thumbs-up. Kylian, who was wearing a Real Madrid tracksuit top, took the photo back to his bedroom in Bondy and put it on the wall.

Naturally, next came the seats in the directors' box. For a match against Espanyol the club made sure he and his family had the best seats in the house.

This was Real Madrid's way of trying to impress Kylian and his family. They wanted to sign him straight away. Zidane and Ronaldo had watched Kylian train for a whole week and they knew he would be a big star.

Kylian's mum and dad, however, wanted him to stay at school and remain close to friends and family in France. They felt that staying at school, playing at Bondy under the watchful eye of his father and being able to play with his friends would help him stay healthy, happy and focused.

Chelsea Trial

When he was eleven Kylian had had a trial at Chelsea. It began a period of Kylian begging his parents to let him leave for a big club in a big city.

His eyes had been opened to possibilities and he was hungry to improve his football education in a foreign country. But his mum and dad knew what was best for him. He had to stay patient.

Kylian had spent a week with Chelsea and he played for their Under-12s team against Charlton, alongside Tammy Abraham, who would go on to play for England. Poor Charlton didn't know what hit them. "I think we won seven or eight nil," Kylian said.

In fact, it was 8–0. Chelsea presented him with a number 10 shirt with KYLIAN on the back. He met Carlo Ancelotti, one of the best football managers ever. He also met Didier Drogba and Florent Malouda, taking pictures on his dad's phone. His Bondy teammates were amazed when they saw the pictures.

But despite his excellent performance, Chelsea asked Kylian to return for another trial. Kylian's mum was furious. She thought that they should have been able to recognise how good a player he was going to be in a week of training. She said they should have made an immediate offer. This turned out for the best, of course, for Kylian – but not Chelsea, who must regret their decision!

As Kylian's time at Clairefontaine was coming to an end, Chelsea still wanted him, but so did every major club in the world, including all the French clubs, Manchester United, Manchester City, Liverpool, Bayern Munich, and, of course, Real. At fifteen, everyone was talking about the boy wonder from Bondy who had amazing skills and speed. It was decision time for Kylian and his family. Which club would win the race for his signature? Amazingly, he almost signed for a club few people had even heard of.

4

THE RACE IS ON

Everyone agreed that stardom beckoned for Kylian when he graduated from Clairefontaine – his coaches, his fellow students, the hundreds of scouts that came to watch him. But Kylian had known it since he was a small boy, so he wasn't worried about finding the right club. He put his faith in his parents.

That's why if they had told him to go to Caen, he would have done. Caen? Who are they? Exactly. They were a small club in Normandy, 125 miles from Paris. They had never won Ligue 1 or even a French cup competition. It was about as unfashionable a club as you can imagine.

When the club contacted Wilfried, Kylian's dad thought it was a joke. "You are trying to catch a whale with a fishing rod," he said.

But Caen knew all about Kylian. They had been watching him since he was twelve, knew his game inside out and knew how to improve him. Unlike most clubs in the race to sign Kylian, Caen had put together a detailed kick-by-kick plan for his career. Wilfried was impressed, and after discussing it as a family, they agreed they would meet with Caen. This was in the early stages of Kylian's Clairefontaine education, when he was thirteen.

Caen told the Mbappés that they would guarantee Kylian would be playing first-team football at the age of sixteen. His father was really pleased – he thought it was crucial for his son's development to play top-flight football as quickly as possible so he could learn to adapt and grow stronger. Indeed, he was so impressed that after a second meeting, they agreed to a deal with Caen before his time at Clairefontaine was up.

However, the move had to be delayed because French league rules meant that clubs couldn't sign young players more than thirty miles from their home. Instead, Kylian would complete his education at Clairefontaine and then join Caen.

Caen Lose Out

It wasn't to be, though, for the small club. They were denied the chance to sign him after they were relegated from Ligue 1 in 2012. Wilfried agreed that if Caen gained promotion the very next season, Kylian would still sign. But they failed and their chance was gone.

Caen falling out of the race put Rennes at the front. They were not a big club with lots of expensive players, but they did have Kylian's brother, Jirès.

Jirès told Kylian that they could play together and score loads of goals and have even more fun in the red shirts of Rennes. Kylian had a trial at the club and, of course, they were desperate to sign him. And he was keen, too, because it was a club which felt like home. From the age of seven he had been in and around the Rennes training ground and players, looking up to his big brother.

It soon became clear to Real Madrid and the other big European clubs that the Mbappé family wanted

Kylian to stay in France and join a club which would be able to fast-track him into the first team. At clubs such as Real and Manchester United, it could be years before he got close to the first team because of the way these clubs used the transfer system. If they had a hole in the team they filled it by signing a player for millions. That was what was required for a team to stay at the top. Rarely did they have the opportunity to let a young player grow.

So Kylian's dream of playing for Real would not be realised. "Maybe later in your career," said his mum.

Instead, Kylian agreed to join AS Monaco, signing a three-year youth contract at the age of fourteen before his time would be up at Clairefontaine a year later. AS Monaco was a club with a rich tradition for developing France's best players. It had an academy which was very similar to Clairefontaine, their scouts knew the Mbappé family well and it was where Thierry Henry had started too!

5

FOOTBALLER FACTORY

AS Monaco was the ideal place for Kylian to develop, and the perfect stepping stone towards realising his ambition.

For a start, he could stay in France and be close to friends and family. Moving to Madrid, to a new city where he didn't know anyone, would have felt like an extra complication.

Most important was the AS Monaco youth academy. It was called La Turbie and it had better facilities than some of the biggest clubs in the world.

Monaco have always taken youth football seriously. In 1987 Arsène Wenger, the famous Arsenal manager, went there and brought to the first team Thierry Henry, Emmanuel Petit and Lilian Thuram. All won the World Cup in 1998, the year Kylian was born. David Trezeguet, the France striker who scored sixty-two goals in 125 matches for his country, was also a Monaco academy graduate. Thierry, Emmanuel and Lilian had joined at the age of fifteen and all played at least 100 matches for Monaco before moving to another team.

With Monaco being such a small place – it has only around 38,000 people living there – the club does not have loads of youngsters in the area to scout. But they have more scouts in the whole of France than any other club, and, amazingly, more scouts in Paris than Paris Saint-Germain. So Monaco knew all about Kylian before anybody else and their scouts were talking with his mum and dad from when he was very young.

Like Caen, Monaco had a plan for Kylian. They would make sure he was fast-tracked into the Under-17s team, and from there he would play for Monaco B. This was Monaco's reserve team. It was proper men's football. Monaco B played in an amateur league but it was a great place for youngsters to get used to the physical side of the sport.

They also had made plans for Kylian to continue his schooling. Monaco employed their own teachers who would visit the club's stadium to hold lessons.

Wilfried was also able to move to Monaco to help his son settle in. The club found father and son a place to live near the training ground while Fayza stayed in Bondy to look after Ethan, who was seven at the time.

When Kylian signed for Monaco, they were a club trying to compete with some of the biggest and richest clubs in the world in the transfer market. Claudio Ranieri, the manager who would later lead Leicester City to their unbelievable Premier League title, was in charge, and thanks to the Russian billionaire owner, Dmitry Rybolovlev, they signed famous players. They wanted to end a thirteen-year wait for the French title.

It was a slight change from their usual style of relying on youngsters. They wanted to blend established superstars with their young talent which was coming through, such as Anthony Martial, who would go on to play for Manchester United. But the club wanted to see what would happen and they knew they had a crop of exciting talent – like Kylian – who would ensure they switched back to their traditions.

Colombian strikers Radamel Falcao and James

Rodríguez had been paired together to score the goals to challenge Paris Saint-Germain in Ligue 1. João Moutinho, the Portugal midfielder, arrived from Porto and his international teammate, the defender Ricardo Carvalho, also signed. France international Eric Abidal, another defender, joined from Barcelona.

Kylian was excited to get going. He and his father discussed what he should try to achieve when at Monaco. They decided he should be in the first team by the end of his three-year youth contract, that he would work hard at school and improve his game. Kylian also added an extra goal for his career at the club: to win Ligue 1. But despite his talent and reputation, Kylian's Monaco career did not get off to a good start.

Frustration

Despite all the planning by his mum and dad, the detailed career path mapped out by Monaco, the hard work of his coaches at Clairefontaine and, of course, his amazing ability, Kylian suffered his first problem in his career in the early days at La Turbie.

The problem seemed to come from one of the

promises that Monaco had made when he signed: that Kylian would go straight into the Under-17s. The coach of the Under-17s, Bruno Irles, did not agree and said that Kylian was not ready. He was in disagreement with the people who ran the club.

Irles thought the Monaco board should not be telling him how to do his job and so was perhaps harder on Kylian than he might have been on players of a similar age. Irles said Kylian did not track back enough to get the ball back in matches. All he wanted to do was go on mazy runs and score goals.

To help him try to learn that lesson, Irles said he wouldn't play him and instead said he should go to play in an amateur league to understand how his game needed to develop if he was going to make it at the top level. It was a shock for Kylian. How had it come to this? The move to Monaco, following in the footsteps of Thierry Henry, was supposed to be perfect. And yet here he was, not even being allowed to play for the youth team he had signed for?

Wilfried was angry because he knew what was happening. He had worked in football for so long and had seen it before. Kylian was caught in the middle of this argument between the coach and the board. Irles was using Kylian to make his point. Wilfried would not stand for it and had a row with Irles. Irles insisted he was just trying to help Kylian improve and he wouldn't pick him until he worked harder on the pitch.

With Kylian increasingly unhappy, Wilfried spoke to the Monaco board. Kylian was brought back from the amateur league and with Irles still refusing to play him, his first season at Monaco ended with him training on his own. It was a disaster.

These days, football insiders believe it was all a clever ploy from Monaco to make Kylian hungrier. They wanted him to feel as if he had worked extra hard. Sure, they knew he had the talent but did he have the desire to go with it? By holding him back they thought they were helping. It sure was a risky policy.

Still, with the football world so small, word soon got out that Kylian was unhappy at Monaco. This led to a number of clubs trying to sign Kylian.

The one club which came closest to taking advantage of Kylian's situation was Arsenal. Arsène Wenger had been alerted.

By the time Wenger spoke to Kylian, things were going much better at Monaco but the legendary Arsenal manager still talks about the one that got away. Wenger met with Kylian and his parents at his home in Bondy in a bid to try to persuade him to leave Monaco and there was even talk of a transfer fee of £230,000. It was low because of rules concerning young players. That would have been one of the biggest bargains in football history.

Monaco's Star Factory – How They Do It

Scouting: Monaco have more scouts than any other team in France, and they are the most qualified. They track players from the age of eleven.

Play everywhere: Youngsters are played in lots of different positions to help them understand the game more. They do this until they are seventeen.

Smartphones: As soon as a match has finished youth players are sent feedback about their performance on their smartphone.

Monaco B: This is Monaco's reserve team. It is a mix of older professional players and the best youngsters. They play in France's fourth league, the highest amateur division. The team gives young players a taste of the physicality of men's football.

6

BACK TO HIS BEST

Kylian's second season at Monaco was much better, largely because the coach who didn't think he was good enough, Bruno Irles, had left. Instead, Kylian was coached by Frédéric Barilaro. Barilaro had no such doubts about Kylian's ability and attidude.

With his confidence restored Kylian was back to his best. He dazzled in the youth teams to the extent that it was decided he should be promoted to the Under-19s team. He ran off the ball to make space for others. He tracked back. He passed when he should pass. He dribbled when he should dribble. And the goals flowed as his finishing skills improved …

BANG! In one match he cleverly darted between the two central defenders, allowed a pass to come across his body and with his right foot he shot it past the keeper.

ZOOM! In another he picked the ball up on the left-winger, outpaced a defender, did a clever stepover to fool another and from a tight angle squeezed the ball into the net.

DINK! Taking a cross from the left Kylian again let the ball roll across his body and with the outside of his right foot he chipped the ball past the despairing dive of the goalkeeper.

All goals were celebrated in the style of his idol, Cristiano Ronaldo – a jump in the air and as he landed, bringing his arms down from a cross position to his sides as if to say, "GAME OVER!"

Kylian's return to form was perfect timing. Monaco had stopped spending big transfer fees on players. Their plan to take on Paris Saint-Germain had failed. The best they had managed was a second-placed finish behind the Paris giants in that 2013–14 season. They were going to need their starlets instead, and one of them in particular. But first they had to persuade him to stay.

Breakthrough

At the start of the 2015–16 season Kylian was sixteen years old. Remember that Caen had promised he would be playing first-team football at that age? Kylian and his family had not forgotten. They were worried that Monaco would not give him a chance in the new campaign.

More big clubs were showing an interest in signing Kylian, particularly after the family's meeting with Arsène Wenger. Paris Saint-Germain were interested. RB Leipzig, the German club, had also emerged as a possible destination. But Kylian and his dad decided that if Kylian left early he could earn a reputation for being a difficult character. They were also aware that if he joined a new club he would have to start from scratch. Trusted family advisors had also warned that the first-team environment at a new club would be harsh. Kylian was still an unknown and senior pros wouldn't give him the time of day.

His brother Jirès had given him advice too: work harder, improve your game, score goals and everything will work out. Well, to Kylian that was easy. He decided to play so well that Monaco would have to pick him for first-team action. He wasted little time in making an impact, scoring ten goals in his first five matches that season for the Under-19s team.

The club's vice president Vadim Vasilyev came to watch Kylian in training. He couldn't believe his eyes. Everything that he had been told was true: Monaco had a goalscoring wonderkid, one with speed, skill and a burning desire to do well.

He immediately set up a meeting with Wilfried and Fayza as he was keen to reassure them that Kylian was a big part of the club's future. They pointed out that Kylian had to be playing first-team football by the end of his three-year youth contract, otherwise they would have to seriously consider moving him. Vasilyev, desperate not to lose their star asset, said, "No problem, he will train with the first team as soon as possible."

When Kylian first stepped on to the training pitch with the first team, he knew his time had come. This was no time to be nervous or afraid. He had to show them what he could do.

Everything clicked for Kylian in that training session. He outpaced all the defenders. He tracked back. He didn't give the ball away. He finished like a player at his peak. It was such a brilliant performance that it was talked about for weeks at the club and it has not been forgotten to this day.

Leonardo Jardim, the first-team manager, also couldn't believe what he had seen. "This boy must not go back to the reserves," he said. Jardim claimed him as one of his own. Kylian was a first-team player now.

It would take only another month before Jardim unleashed Kylian Mbappé on the professional football world. But few who saw it would have predicted how he was going to take the world by storm after a low-key debut on a chilly Wednesday night in December 2015.

There were only a few thousand fans in Monaco's home stadium, the Stade Louis II, for the match against Caen, the club which had come close to signing Kylian from Clairefontaine.

Monaco had been winning the game 1–0 until the eighty-sixth minute when Caen managed an equaliser. Jardim thought it was the ideal time to try Kylian. It was a low-pressure game, the defenders were tired, and if he put Kylian on the young man would be a record breaker.

With eighteen days to go until his seventeenth birthday, Kylian would be the youngest ever to don the famous red and white shirt of Monaco. The previous holder of the record? Thierry Henry. Monaco and Kylian both wanted this record to change hands. For Monaco, it would further improve their reputation as a club which produced excellent talent. For Kylian, well, he always knew he was going to be a record breaker.

And so in the eighty-eighth minute Kylian was told, "It's time." He took off his tracksuit, after doing some quick sprints down the touchline to warm up, and waited for Fábio Coentrão to shake hands with him before Fabio came off and Kylian replaced him. Kylian was told to try to cause as much damage as possible.

In the end he got few touches on the ball. He had one dangerous run which Caen did well to halt with a well-timed tackle. It was a glimpse of the blistering speed which would soon be terrorising defenders. Kylian knew it was just the start. He left the field disappointed, though, wishing he had scored and that Monaco had won the match.

Scaring Spurs

For Monaco's next match, against Bastia, Kylian had to make do with a place on the bench again. With the match in the balance, Jardim was reluctant to risk him and he didn't go on. Monaco scored twice in the last eighteen minutes to take the win.

But he did come off the bench in their next match. It was away to Tottenham Hotspur in the Europa League, the sort of occasion that Kylian had dreamed of being involved in and knew he belonged at. He came on after fifty-six minutes with Monaco 3–0 down. He needed five minutes to make an impact.

When he was passed the ball on the left wing, Kylian immediately had the full-back back-pedalling furiously. He turned his rival inside out with two magical stepovers, and with the Tottenham defence keen to get two players to tackle him he had managed to do something his coaches had always told him to think about: find space for others. With Tottenham panicking, Kylian's sharp pass found Stephan El Shaarawy, who curled a brilliant shot into the net.

The full-back, by the way, was Kieran Trippier,

who would go on to star for England in the 2018 World Cup.

For the rest of the match Kylian was a constant threat with fast, direct running and tricks. On that performance he should have been playing from the start. Manager Jardim didn't disagree. In Monaco's next match but one, away to Bordeaux, Kylian was in the starting XI. But it was a bad day for the team as they lost 3–0, although Kylian once again gave notice that he was dangerous.

Kylian had made a strong impression, but Jardim wanted him to do more work on his game with the reserves. He was told that there was no rush and they planned to bring him back into the squad in a few games' time. Kylian worked harder than ever before and he was back on the substitutes bench against Toulouse in January 2016. Both Monaco and Kylian had an eye on another record: Monaco's youngest ever goalscorer.

History Boy

In the third match after his return to the first team, Kylian made history. Monaco were winning

2–1 against Troyes. Kylian had come on in the seventy-third minute. He had been as electric as ever and the Monaco fans were now well aware they had someone very special to cheer on. The clock had ticked over into the ninety-third minute. Troyes were pushing for an equalising goal but carelessly gave the ball away, letting Hélder Costa run towards goal. He crossed from the left and there were two Monaco players racing to meet the ball … Kylian and Tiémoué Bakayoko.

But Tiémoué didn't have Kylian's pace and he couldn't match his desire for his first goal. Kylian sprinted to connect with the pass and without slowing down or steadying himself, struck a perfect left-footed shot over the helpless keeper into the net. YES! Kylian Mbappé had arrived. And smashed another record. He was Monaco's youngest ever goalscorer at the age of seventeen years and sixty-two days, beating, you guessed it, Thierry Henry.

He was so happy, Kylian ran off with his arms stretched out like a plane. He felt like he was flying. His teammates came over to hug him. After the congratulations, Kylian did a cool dance and gave a thumbs-up to the crowd.

For the rest of the season, Kylian started one more match (against Nantes) and made five more substitute appearances, including away to Paris Saint-Germain in a brilliant 2–0 win for Monaco. It helped Monaco to finish third in the 2015–16 season and ensure they qualified for the Champions League – and that was crucial in helping to persuade Kylian to sign for Monaco again.

On 7 March 2016 Kylian agreed a three-year contract. His first proper professional deal. Club president Vadim Vasilyev said Kylian was "a player of great talent".

He was right, of course. And Monaco's timing was perfect, not just because the big clubs were trying to convince him to leave. That summer Kylian would boost his reputation further.

7

EURO STAR

A lot had happened in a short space of time for Kylian. He had established himself as a first-team squad member at Monaco and signed his first professional contract. This was no surprise to those who knew about French football. His name was known. In the summer of 2016, he made sure the whole of Europe knew who he was.

Kylian was the star of the European Under-19 Championship in Germany. He produced sizzling performances which are still talked about. One European football scout said: “He bossed the whole tournament.”

But he almost didn't play. Despite success at academies and his clubs, Kylian had rarely represented France's youth teams. He had played twice for the Under-17s. The Under-18s coach, Jean-Claude Giuntini, seemed to have a grudge against Kylian and said he didn't work hard enough for the team.

It was strange because most coaches who worked with Kylian and most scouts who watched him all reported that his attitude was flawless. Unfortunately, though, the opinions of a tiny number of coaches, and that difficult start at Monaco, had denied him matches for France. He had, amazingly, been left out of the France squad for the European Under-17 Championship in 2015, a tournament they won.

Unsurprisingly, the seventeen-year-old Kylian wasted little time in proving his doubters wrong. He was a key player as France qualified for the tournament when they needed to win their last three matches. He was full of wonderful running and mazy dribbling in a victory over Montenegro. He then scored in a 4–0 beating of Denmark.

In the final match, against Serbia, the pressure was on. France had to win.

Kylian was everywhere. He played on the right

wing. He played on the left. Both full-backs were given a difficult time. He picked up the ball in central midfield and tried to play the strikers through on goal. He had a shot cleared off the line. At times he was playing them on his own. So it was no surprise he hit the winning goal, just before half-time.

Jean-Kévin Augustin, the striker, played a neat pass to Kylian on the right-hand side of the area. Kylian shimmied, found space and unleashed a shot which beat the goalkeeper at his near post. Brilliant.

Jean-Kévin and Kylian combining would be a sign of things to come. Coach Batelli knew he had a special duo on his hands.

France were one of the favourites to win the tournament, which was held in Germany. But their campaign got off to a bad start when they were beaten 2–1 by England. Kylian was subbed off in the second half as he struggled with England's physicality. Jean-Kévin scored the goal for France.

In the next match, however, both Kylian and Jean-Kévin were on the scoresheet as they beat Croatia 2–0. It was the start of Jean-Kévin and Kylian having their own personal goalscoring battle. Who could score most?

The final group match was one France could not afford to lose. There was no danger of that, though, as Kylian and Jean-Kévin ran riot. Kylian scored twice but Jean-Kévin notched one more for a hat-trick! France qualified for the semi-finals in second position from their group, behind England.

Destroyer

Kylian took centre stage in the semis against Portugal. He destroyed them on his own, scoring two goals and setting up the other. And all of that after France had gone behind in the third minute.

The equaliser came in the tenth minute. Kylian had the ball near the corner flag on the left wing with two Portugal players surrounding him. *Easy*, he thought. A few tricks and a burst of pace later and he was in the box, squaring the ball for Ludovic Blas to tap home.

Throughout the game Kylian was a menace. His feet were so fast they were a blur and the poor Portuguese defenders couldn't cope. After a flashing stepover one stumbled and fell in a heap. He was beating the Portuguese at will, playing in his teammates for chances and shooting from distance himself.

His two goals were actually rather simple. A tap-in from a right-wing cross and then a cute flicked header from a corner. "He's had a great game," the commentator said. That was an understatement.

In the final against Italy Kylian made gaps for his teammates just by being on the pitch. It was an easy win for France as Jean-Kévin scored the first of four goals. Kylian was desperate to get on the scoresheet but it wasn't to be as his friend pipped him by one goal to end up with six for the tournament.

In the stands watching with his parents was Atmane Airouche, the president of Bondy. He was very proud to see the boy from Bondy shining on such an important stage. But something surprised him.

"We met him outside the stadium and we were shocked that he didn't want to go partying with his teammates," he said. "Instead he wanted to go straight home. To him, he had achieved his goal to be European champion and was already thinking about his next goal: going back to Monaco, getting into their team, winning more titles."

8

MONACO MARVEL

Remember when Kylian first signed for Monaco aged fourteen? He didn't just want to break through into the first team, he wanted to win the league title. So as the 2016–17 season began for Monaco, Kylian's head was full of dreams of lifting the trophy. And why not? He had just played for France's Under-19s and was the biggest and brightest young star in Europe.

But Kylian came back to earth with a bump. In Monaco's first match of the season against Guingamp, he suffered a nasty head injury and had to come off. Monaco were losing 2–0 at the time. His replacement,

Bernardo Silva, helped turn the game around and it was Silva who equalised in the eighty-fourth minute.

From then on, Valère Germain was preferred to Kylian as Monaco couldn't stop winning. After the Guingamp match, they won seven matches in a row, including a 2–1 victory over Tottenham in the Champions League. Even Paris Saint-Germain were beaten, in an amazing 3–1 win for Monaco. Kylian didn't even make the squad for those two games and until he returned to the starting XI against Montpellier almost six long weeks later, he had played only twenty-eight minutes off the bench in three games.

Kylian was, of course, frustrated. But he knew it was really hard for a manager to change a winning team, let alone a strike force that was doing so well. Instead he worked harder than ever in training, recognising that in his first full season with the first team there was still plenty to learn.

So when his chance came against Montpellier, Kylian was ready. He won Monaco a penalty. Four minutes into the second half, Kylian showed exactly how hard he had been working with a style of goal that he was not known for, a deft header from a sweeping cross from the right. He had outmuscled the defender to grab a yard of space and leapt high, glancing the ball back into the net. Monaco went on to win the match 6–2.

They didn't look back. Nor did Kylian. Three games later Kylian scored against Nancy. Three games after that he scored against Bastia. He had found his feet in the first team. Monaco's fans were full of praise for their brilliant young striker. Not only was he scoring goals but he was showing pace and skill on the ball. Sooner or later, everyone at Monaco felt, Kylian was going to destroy a team.

Hat-trick Hero

Poor Rennes would be that team on a Wednesday night in December in the French Cup. After twenty-one minutes, Kylian had secured the match for Monaco, having scored twice. The first goal was a carefully placed left-foot shot from the edge of the area. The second was all about blistering pace. Freed down the left-hand side, Kylian raced towards the goal and sent a shot into the far corner with his right foot. With almost seventy minutes left could he claim his first professional hat-trick?

Absolutely. The third goal arrived in the sixty-first minute and it completed what many onlookers thought was a complete hat-trick, displaying a full range of skills. His first two goals had been about precision and power with left and right foot. This one was cheeky and clever. Played in on goal with the goalkeeper rushing out and defenders lurking, Kylian had to think fast on his feet. He managed to get a right-footed clip away just in time.

As a sign of how much he had grown up, Kylian did not celebrate in the style of his idol Cristiano Ronaldo. He was his own man now. He punched the air and nodded his head as if to say, "This is where I belong!"

Monaco won the match 7–0. It was their seventy-sixth goal in twenty-eight matches. Monaco ended the year on a seemingly unstoppable charge to the league title. Yet Kylian was only just warming up.

In February, after a crucial strike against Montpellier in a 2–1 win, he made history again in the next contest against Metz. Another hat-trick. Kylian had been in devastating form from kick-off but even those who knew of his talent were amazed at how quickly he scored three goals. It only took him fifty minutes. At eighteen years and two months he became the youngest player ever to score a hat-trick in Ligue 1.

In his next seven games, Kylian scored seven goals. And one of them was very special indeed.

9

CITY STUNNER

When Kylian and his family were worrying about whether Kylian should move early from Monaco or not, a scout told them that if he walked into a different first-team dressing room they would say, "Who are you?"

Well, after his goalscoring glut every dressing room in Europe knew who Kylian was. He had earned his stripes in men's football and he had proven his doubters wrong.

Monaco coach Leonardo Jardim had been hugely impressed by Kylian's play. So it was time to unleash him from the start on the biggest stage possible: the Champions League.

And against Manchester City no less, managed by the legend that is Pep Guardiola. It is crazy to think that Kylian was only eighteen years old when Jardim pulled him to one side in training in the days before the game and said, "You are starting against Manchester City." Even crazier to think that Kylian was not in the least bit nervous. Instead he told his manager that it was a decision he wouldn't regret.

Earlier in the season Kylian had made two Champions League appearances, but both were off the bench, against CSKA Moscow and Bayer Leverkusen. In Manchester, he would play from the start in one of the biggest stadiums in Europe, in front of more than 50,000 fans and against some of the world's best defenders.

There were still no nerves from Kylian as he and his Monaco teammates took to the pitch. Kylian was desperate to do well and had been told to attack-attack-attack down Manchester City's left side. Coach Jardim thought City were weak there and Kylian would make hay.

He was right. With the game poised at 1–1 after Radamel Falcao had equalised Raheem Sterling's goal, Kylian's pace and positivity brought him a chance. He outpaced the legend Yaya Touré but fired his shot wide. *Next time*, Kylian seemed to be saying to himself. He then bamboozled Nicolás Otamendi with a brilliant turn. Then he fooled the defender again, nutmegging him and leaving him in a heap on the turf.

In the fortieth minute, Kylian gave Monaco a sensational lead. And it was all down to his speed and brains. A clipped pass in behind the City defence looked harmless but Kylian burst through a gap, spinning off the shoulder of poor Nicolás again. Suddenly in a blur, Kylian was in on goal and the ball was in the back of the net.

"MMM-BA-PAY!" screamed the commentator.

At eighteen years and two months Kylian was the second-youngest Frenchman to score in the Champions League. The youngest was Karim Benzema. Not bad company, was it?

Kylian should have had another goal in the second half as City and Monaco traded goals in a thrilling game. It would finish 5–3 to City but Monaco were far from disheartened. They had scored crucial away goals, which would make a difference if the scores were level on aggregate (the total number of goals scored in both games). City were disappointed. And a little afraid. What would Kylian do to them next time?

City were right to be worried. In the second leg it took only six minutes for Kylian to fire a warning shot. Again, from nowhere, he outpaced the City defence, getting in on goal only for goalkeeper Willy Caballero to make a fine save. Less than two minutes later Kylian found the net with a poacher's goal. He instinctively stuck out a leg to turn home Bernardo Silva's smash across goal. Monaco were only a goal behind.

They continued to attack the City goal with Kylian playing brilliantly. In the thirty-first minute they went 2–0 up and made it 5–5 on aggregate with Fabinho slotting home. Even Leroy Sané pulling a goal back and putting City into an overall lead of 6–5 couldn't halt Monaco's charge. They scored again seven minutes later for a 3–1 win on the night and a 6–6 tie over the two legs. Those three goals in Manchester, including Kylian's, were enough for them to progress.

Monaco seemed unstoppable. They were hailed as the most exciting team in the tournament. And Kylian was their driving force. The newspapers, playing catch-up, called him the new Thierry Henry.

France legend Robert Pires was one of the first to compare Kylian to Thierry Henry. "I had the pleasure of playing with Henry and I can tell you he was doing the same things at [Kylian's age]. They're the same players. He's going to keep improving and he'll have a great career."

The Famous Celebration

In the quarter-finals against German giants Borussia Dortmund, Kylian saw them off on his own. Dortmund were scared of Kylian's pace and he won Monaco a penalty with a burst which left them standing. But oh no! Fabinho missed, his shot going wide of the left-hand post.

It didn't matter, though. Kylian turned in a cross with his thigh to give them the lead in the nineteenth minute. It seemed a lucky goal but Kylian didn't care as he slid across the grass on his knees. "Yes!" he said.

Unfortunately, Monaco's defence made a mistake, even after an own goal had given Monaco a two-goal cushion. It was 2-1 heading into the final stages. Kylian was stalking the Dortmund defence, waiting for any error – and in the seventy-ninth minute they made one. A loose pass was pounced on by Kylian. He could have a clear run on goal if he wanted. Instead he took the ball a few yards and unleashed a shot from outside the area high into the net.

Kylian slid away on his knees and for the first time fans glimpsed what would be an iconic celebration. He folded his arms across his chest as if to say 'job done'. As Kylian had been smashing goals in left, right and centre for months, his younger brother Ethan had told him that Kylian needed to have his own celebration. He was now too famous to be copying Ronaldo's.

But even this wasn't his own – Kylian had borrowed it from Ethan. This was how the kid would celebrate when he scored a goal against his older brother when playing *FIFA*. Kylian liked the celebration, though, because it was a way to show Ethan he was thinking of him even in the biggest games in Europe.

And there would be more to come. In the second leg of the quarter-final, Dortmund were beaten 3–1 with Kylian again on the scoresheet. It set up a

Champions League semi-final with Juventus. Wow. How far had Kylian come in such a short time? He was tingling with excitement as he walked out against the famous Italian team.

But sadly, Juventus were too strong in the first leg at Monaco's ground. Their experienced and hardened players had too many tricks for Monaco's youngsters and they won 2–0. Kylian briefly gave Monaco hope in the second leg with a sixty-ninth-minute goal but it wasn't to be.

Never mind, Kylian thought. *One day I will win the Champions League*. It had always been his ambition. But before that, he knew he was more likely to realise his goal of winning the French title. And with six goals in eight games, Kylian was in perfect form to make history.

10

TITLE JOY

Paris Saint-Germain had been breathing down their necks in Ligue 1 all season. And Monaco, despite putting together winning runs consistently – they had won eight in a row as a crucial match against Lille approached – couldn't quite shake them off. But they knew if they kept winning, PSG would not catch them.

Lille were tough opponents but if Monaco beat them they would then only have to beat Saint-Étienne, in the second from last game of the season, to confirm the title.

There were no nerves in the Monaco dressing

room. How could there be? They had proved to be one of the best teams in Europe. And they came flying at Lille as soon as the first whistle went. Predictably, Kylian led the way with darting runs. Radamel Falcao scored after only six minutes for a 1–0 lead.

On the stroke of half-time, Kylian put the game beyond doubt with a mazy bit of skill and dribbling to cross for Bernardo Silva. For good measure, Kylian made the third for Radamel as Monaco went on to win 4–0. Now they just needed to beat Saint-Étienne in front of their home crowd to win their first title since 2000, when Kylian was just a year old!

And you just know who scored the opening goal to set Monaco on their way … Kylian! It was a trademark Kylian goal. A pass through the middle gave the Saint-Étienne defence no chance of keeping up with him. He could have shot first time but instead Kylian thought he'd have some fun and dribble around the goalkeeper. For a second it looked as though he had taken the ball too wide but, cool as you like, he slotted the ball home. And to celebrate? The trademark Kylian celebration at the corner flag, arms across chest and a nod of the head.

Monaco won 2–0 and the title was theirs. Cue

epic celebrations on the pitch in front of a packed stadium! Kylian was ecstatic as he watched the fans celebrating, waving their huge red and white flags.

The Next Messi

In Monaco's title-winning season, Kylian was scoring or making a goal every sixty-five minutes. Only Lionel Messi had a better record than that in Europe's top five leagues.

Taking it Easy

Kylian could have gone to a hundred parties that night but instead he went home to be with his family. He wanted to think about what he had achieved. When he arrived at Monaco he said he wanted to be in the first team after three seasons. He was. He also said he wanted to be a Ligue 1 winner. He was.

There were the records and the awards too. When he passed fifteen goals for the season at the age of eighteen years and 147 days, he became the youngest in more than 100 years to manage such a tally in the top divisions of France, England, Germany, Italy and Spain. In league and cups he had scored twenty-six times and made eleven more goals. He was named as the fourth-best forward in Europe by UEFA, with his idol Cristiano Ronaldo winning. He also made the UEFA team of the season and won the Ligue 1 Young Player of the Year award.

A lesser-known achievement was passing his school exams! Kylian earned a qualification in management of science and technology. It was just as he promised his parents. When Kylian put his mind to something, on the pitch or not, he achieved.

His joy was tinged with sadness, though, because he knew he might be leaving Monaco.

All the biggest clubs in the world positioned themselves on the starting line in the race to sign Kylian. And the price was about to go up.

11

LES BLEUS

Kylian could have played international football for Cameroon because that's where his dad was from. Or he could have chosen Algeria because of his mum. A boy in a hurry could easily have been swayed by the certainty that both of those countries would have made him one of the youngest international players ever. Either would have been the easy, quick fix. But Kylian wasn't interested in doing things the easy way.

France was the only country he wanted to represent. And he didn't just want to play for Les Bleus, he wanted to star for them and win European

Championships and World Cups. Those were his goals. As he always said to his father, "You have to aim as high as possible."

Didier Deschamps, the France manager, loved this attitude. So as soon as he got the chance to pick Kylian, he did. In March 2017 Kylian was named in the senior squad. This was instead of going to the Under-20 World Cup with France in South Korea. He immediately wowed more experienced teammates. Olivier Giroud couldn't believe how mature and confident he was.

Kylian made his debut against Luxembourg on 25 March, coming off the bench. At eighteen years, three months and five days he was the second-youngest ever to play for his country. Another record. But he was disappointed that day – he should have scored with his first touch of the ball, the goalkeeper pulling off a brilliant save.

Too fast!

Three days later he started his first match for France. And against the mighty Spain, no less. He had some good moments in the game, showing signs of his speed and skills, but it was in his second start that he really impressed – against England in a friendly in

June. This was the game when Monaco began to add extra millions to his transfer price.

Kylian tormented England alongside fellow youth star Ousmane Dembélé. But no one should have been surprised. In the England defence that day was Manchester City's John Stones, whom Kylian had outplayed in those famous games for Monaco in the Champions League. Kieran Trippier, someone Kylian had fooled against Tottenham Hotspur early in his career, was also playing. Kylian was too fast, too positive and too tricky – in one dribble he did a stepover so quickly that Kieran almost fell over!

Kylian hit the bar and had a certain goal denied by goalkeeper Tom Heaton, who stuck out a right leg to stop the ball nestling in the corner. France won 3–2. The margin of victory would have been bigger had Raphaël Varane not been sent off.

It was a significant performance from Kylian coming against England. Sure, they were not an international powerhouse, but as one of the most famous teams, people took notice. The big English clubs like Arsenal, Liverpool and Manchester United needed no further proof Kylian was the real deal. They all wanted him, but there were only two clubs in the race and one was in pole position.

12

THIS TIME FOR REAL?

On a swelteringly hot Monaco summer's day in 2017, a luxurious private jet waited on the tarmac to fly the second-most expensive footballer of all time to join his new teammates on a pre-season tour in Miami. Real Madrid thought they had their man. The Spanish giants were putting the final touches on a deal which would see them unite Kylian and his idol, Cristiano Ronaldo, in the famous white strip.

The fee would be £161 million. Monaco had reluctantly agreed to sell. They knew they couldn't keep Kylian forever and the Madrid offer was far too big to turn down. Amazingly, though, there was a problem, one which few could have predicted: Kylian didn't want to join Real.

Despite admitting that playing for Real was one of his goals, despite the chance to play alongside Ronaldo and despite the prospect of a Champions League winner's medal, Kylian said there was no need for the plane. What had happened?

Firstly, Kylian had not been convinced that he would play every week. When he was speaking to coach Zinedine Zidane, Kylian was surprised to be told that Ronaldo, Karim Benzema, the France striker, and Gareth Bale would still be the preferred front three. The prospect of being frustrated and angry in Madrid, a long way from his family, meant Kylian said no.

Did this let in the likes of Liverpool, Manchester United and Arsenal? Well, Kylian's dad spoke to them all. But going to England was never a realistic option. Wilfried was just being smart by understanding exactly what Kylian's options were.

Instead, it was Paris Saint-Germain who held all the cards. And in fact, they had done for a long, long time. The key was Wilfried's friendship with

Marc Westerloppe, PSG's head of recruitment. Westerloppe had known Wilfried for years and Kylian's dad trusted him so much he had almost arranged for his son to sign for RC Lens when he was younger because Westerloppe worked there.

"Come and Join Me"

Westerloppe set up a meeting at Kylian's family home on 7 July. Unai Emery, the PSG manager, was there and assured Kylian that he would be first choice. They told him that he would likely be playing alongside Neymar, the brilliant Brazil forward. PSG were also in talks to sign him from Barcelona.

Kylian remained unsure, however. He was excited about the prospect of a new season with Monaco. They had such great players! Maybe he could win the Champions League with them? PSG didn't give up. In fact, once they had signed Neymar they told him to send Kylian text messages. "Come and join me! We will score loads of goals."

In the end, Monaco took the decision out of Kylian's hands. They had financial worries and needed the money. They had also sold Bernardo Silva and Benjamin Mendy to Manchester City. Monaco's amazing team was being broken up.

As pre-season began, PSG agreed an initial loan deal so they would not break financial fair play rules. They would pay £122 million with another £40 million due in bonuses. Kylian would earn more than £18 million a year, the highest salary ever for an eighteen-year-old.

Most Expensive Footballers

Neymar: Barcelona to Paris Saint-Germain €222m 2017

Kylian Mbappé: Monaco to Paris Saint-Germain €185m 2017

João Félix: Benfica to Atlético Madrid €126m 2019

Philippe Coutinho: Liverpool to Barcelona €160m 2018

Antoine Griezmann: Atlético Madrid to Barcelona €120m 2019

Kylian's big move was announced in the final few hours of that summer's transfer window. It also happened to be the day that Kylian would score his first international goal, against Holland in Paris.

When he was unveiled as a PSG player six days after that goal against the Netherlands, he said: "It was important for me to stay in France. I wanted to come back home, to the town where I grew up. With hard work we'll be able to achieve our goal of winning lots of trophies, including the club's ultimate dream: the Champions League."

FOOTBALL LEGENDS

13

THE MCN

Before Monaco's Kylian-inspired stunning title success, Paris Saint-Germain had been the all-conquering force in French football. They had won the league for four years in a row. It was a no-brainer for them to sign Kylian. With one cheque they strengthened themselves and weakened their nearest challengers.

And with another cheque, they had done the same to their European rivals. Neymar's arrival from Barcelona was a clear sign of intent and motivated by revenge. Barcelona had humiliated PSG in the Champions League the previous season. They had to add the Champions League to their domestic success. A strike force of Kylian, Neymar and Edinson Cavani, the striker from Uruguay, was one of the most fearsome ever seen. They would be known as 'the MCN'.

Unsurprisingly, the MCN wasted little time in proving that they would be too good for their French rivals. By the time Kylian made his debut five games into the season against Metz, PSG had won their first four games and scored fourteen goals. PSG would win thirteen of their first fifteen league games. Naturally, Kylian scored on his debut.

PSG also started the Champions League in blistering form. They beat Scottish giants Celtic 5–0 in their first game of the qualifying group in Glasgow with Kylian on the scoresheet. It was merely a warning shot to the rest of the continent. Bayern Munich were dismissed 3–0 in Paris, Celtic were again thrashed out of sight 7–1 (Kylian scored again) while Anderlecht were beaten 9–0 on aggregate.

At Christmas, PSG were top of Ligue 1. They had a nine-point gap to Monaco, in second place. The strike force of Kylian, Neymar and Edinson had scored thirty-eight goals between them.

They were also through to the round of sixteen

of the Champions League, despite a loss to Bayern in the final group game. PSG's MCN had scored twenty-five times in six games. Kylian had scored PSG's only goal in the Bayern loss but had taken away another record – at eighteen years, eleven months and five days he became the youngest player to score ten Champions League goals. The record had previously belonged to Karim Benzema of Real Madrid.

And guess which team PSG were drawn against in their next match? Real, the twelve-time Champions League winners.

Face to Face with His Idol

It was a match which the whole world was excited about. Two of the most powerful clubs in Europe, plus the added spice of Kylian going up against the team which had come so close to signing him in the summer and his first on-pitch meeting with his hero, Cristiano Ronaldo. But as the media whipped themselves into a frenzy about the clash, Kylian did not play along. In fact, quite the opposite. He said: "I loved him when I was little but that is finished." Wow. He meant business.

And he had to. It didn't get much bigger than a Champions League knockout match at the intimidating Bernabéu. There were almost 80,000 packed into the famous stadium. Was Kylian nervous? No chance. After all, he'd been to the Bernabéu as a boy and it was Real who had been so desperate to sign him. He had never felt so confident.

Kylian was revelling playing on such an important stage. The defenders were wary of him and a hush came over the crowd when he got the ball because the Real fans were scared too. And at twenty-one minutes he showed why. Picking up the ball on the right, Kylian found space for a wicked cross, which was eventually met by Adrien Rabiot, who found the net.

Real equalised through a Ronaldo penalty but Kylian almost restored the lead twice. He had a rasping shot saved and then was inches away from connecting with a left-field cross. He slid on the turf but couldn't reach the ball for a tap-in. So close!

Unfortunately PSG lost concentration. In the last eight minutes they not only conceded once but twice. It was a disaster. They had given Real a two-goal start in the second leg.

The MCN remained confident. *If anyone can*

do it, it's us. For the first half, PSG threatened but Real's defence stood firm. Kylian was the first to break through just before half-time. But instead of squaring the ball to Cavani who had an easy tap-in, Kylian chose to shoot. Saved! He buried his face in his hands. It was a reminder that even Kylian could make a mistake and set the tone for the game as Real went on to win 2–1.

PSG did win the league title easily, though. Their total silverware haul included the Coupe de France, Coupe de la Ligue and Trophée des Champions. Kylian scored twenty-one goals in forty-three games in that domestic treble, earning him another Ligue 1 Young Player of the Year award and the Golden Boy trophy. At home, and in Europe, Kylian had proved he was ready for the grandest stage of all: the World Cup Finals.

14

WATCH OUT WORLD

There was never any doubt that Kylian would be named in France's twenty-three-man squad to go to Russia to try to win a second World Cup. But Kylian didn't want to leave it to chance.

In a friendly match against Russia in Moscow, he made sure he would be on that plane. He scored twice. The second was a brilliant goal. Kylian dribbled into the left-hand side of the Russian penalty area and, in a blur, dragged the ball over his heel, flashed two stepovers to make space for the shot and fired home at the near post. Coach Didier Deschamps had seen enough. He took Kylian off – why risk an injury at this stage? – and gave him a congratulatory hug.

France's strength in depth was revealed when the squad was named. There was no room for Karim Benzema or Alexandre Lacazette. Kylian was, of course, included. He was ecstatic. "My first World Cup! My dream!" he said on social media. Best of all, he was given the number 10 shirt. This was a huge honour as it was the same number that Zinedine Zidane had worn

Being part of a World Cup squad was like nothing Kylian had experienced before. When they arrived at their hotel in Istra, Moscow, the hotel staff clapped and cheered. They were each given a Russian doll and the doors to their room had been personalised with painted images of them. Kylian's showed him punching the air. His huge bed had his name on and there were pictures of Kylian playing for France on the walls. They had also been given PlayStations!

In the first game against Australia, Kylian had to pinch himself about what was happening. In the tunnel he looked over at Ousmane Dembélé. They smiled at each other and shook their heads.

Kylian said to him: "Look at us. The boy from

Évreux and the boy from Bondy. We are playing at the World Cup."

"I swear, it's unbelievable," said Ousmane

Kylian walked out onto the pitch and said he felt he had 65 million French people behind him. When he heard 'La Marseillaise', the French national anthem, he almost cried.

Work Harder

France did not start the tournament with the performance they wanted. They beat Australia 2–1 but had needed an eightieth-minute own goal to win. Didier Deschamps, the manager, was furious. And one player in particular had angered him: Kylian!

Deschamps called a team meeting to discuss the performance. He said that Australia's players had worked harder, run further and ran faster. Australia did twice as many sprints as France's players and Kylian had done fewest of anybody. "I thought speed was your strength," Deschamps said to Kylian.

Kylian said he would do better. He wouldn't make

the same error again. Deschamps made sure of that too. In training he was on Kylian's case constantly: track back, make space for others, use your left foot, don't give the ball away. But Kylian didn't mind. He knew Deschamps was just trying to help him and he loved him for it. He would say of his coach: "I would die on the pitch for him."

In the next match against Peru, Kylian made amends. His thirty-fourth-minute goal was enough for the victory. It was another record! The youngest France player to score at a major tournament!

It wasn't a fluent performance from France but few could complain with two wins from two matches. It meant that in their final match against Denmark, victory was not essential. Deschamps decided to rest players, including Kylian, for the knockout matches to come. They played out a dull 0–0 draw. The France fans in the stadium were furious. They booed the players at full time and the media were critical of Deschamps. France were boring and predictable. Why weren't they thrashing teams when they had such exciting players like Kylian, Antoine Griezmann and Paul Pogba?

Deschamps knew what he was doing, though. He

was making sure the team were organised and the players were tracking back. There would come a time to unleash their full potential – and that time was against Argentina in the last sixteen.

Destroying Argentina

It was a blockbuster of a match! Two former World Champions going head to head for a place in the quarter-finals. And Kylian versus Lionel Messi. The boy who would be king against the thirty-one-year-old master.

Kylian and his French teammates were pumped up. Before the game Paul Pogba had given an inspiring speech. "I am not going home tonight!" he shouted. "I am NOT going home!"

Deschamps had reminded Kylian that speed was his greatest asset. Their defenders were not fast enough to stop him, he said. Deschamps was right.

As soon as he got the chance Kylian attacked them with speed. He tried to get right through the middle of the defence but two Argentina players brought him down as he was about to go into the penalty area. The resulting free kick almost brought a goal – Antoine Griezmann smashing a shot against the bar.

Kylian hit top speed minutes later. He picked the ball up outside France's penalty area and had only one thing on his mind: a goal! He flashed past three Argentina players immediately. Kylian was going all the way! They gave chase but could not get near him. Kylian then zoomed past a fourth player, Marcos Rojo. Marcos couldn't catch him and so as Kylian entered the Argentina box, he fouled him. Penalty!

Antoine scored to give France the lead but the tone had been set for the game. Argentina were scared of Kylian. And why not? That run for the penalty was later timed at 37kph, which was as fast as Usain Bolt. Every time he got the ball he threatened them so they fouled him. It disrupted France's play and two goals either side of half-time gave Argentina an unlikely lead.

France did not panic, though. Eleven minutes later they were level with a brilliant strike from full-back Benjamin Pavard. Argentina were beginning to tire. Kylian sensed his chance.

The goal that gave France the lead would have

been nothing more than a half-chance to most ordinary players. But Kylian's quick feet wrong-footed the defenders in a packed penalty box after he controlled a cross. The space he found gave the chance to shoot. Bang! Into the net from a tight angle. France led 3–2!

Kylian's destruction of Argentina's World Cup dreams was complete four minutes later. Olivier Giroud passed across the box to Kylian, who was approaching at top speed. He hit it first time. Goal!

The world was stunned by the nineteen-year-old's performance. "Watch out world, there's a new number ten!" screamed football commentators, pointing out that Lionel Messi also wears the number. "Mbappé destroys Argentina!" "The boy wonder! He's going to be a world beater."

Those two goals made Kylian the first teenager to score twice in a World Cup game since a seventeen-year-old Pelé in 1958. The Brazilian legend tweeted: "Congratulations, @KMbappe. 2 goals in a World Cup so young puts you in great company!"

On to the Final

In the quarter-final against Uruguay, Deschamps made sure France returned to a more disciplined way of playing. Uruguay were so concerned about Kylian that just his presence on the pitch made space for others. France won 2–0. It was a comfortable win rather than a spectacular one.

Kylian did not score and was not as threatening but he probably should have had a goal early on, sending a header over the bar.

It seemed inevitable that France would make the final. They could do it all – be hard to score against and, like a flick of a switch, turn into the most dangerous attacking team. They met Belgium in the semi-final. They were a formidable opponent, probably tougher than Argentina.

Belgium thought it was their best chance to win a World Cup. They had star players such as Eden Hazard, Romelu Lukaku, Vincent Kompany and Kevin De Bruyne. Most teams would be nervous about facing such talent. Not Kylian. On the plane journey to St Petersburg for the biggest game of his life, Kylian fell asleep!

He was right not to worry. France won 1–0 in a game which did not live up to the hype. Again, Kylian missed an early chance but he didn't care – he was going to the World Cup Final! "What a dream!" he wrote on his Instagram page. Croatia and their brilliant playmaker Luka Modrić stood between France and glory.

15

CHAMPION OF THE WORLD

Waiting in the tunnel before the final Kylian nodded and smiled at Ousmane Dembélé again. But he had also been thinking back to that fateful Wednesday in the Coupe 93 final in the stadium in Gagny when, aged eleven, he was scared of failure, earning a telling off from his mum. He had come a long way. *This is no time to be nervous*, he thought. *Enjoy it!*

The best way for Kylian to relax and enjoy the biggest match in the world was to get on the ball and hurt Croatia. He got straight on with it, getting into the penalty area down the right side and almost finding a teammate with a cross. He then sprinted with the ball towards the goal, only to be stopped by a tackle. Almost!

Antoine Griezmann was having more luck and was causing Croatia all sorts of problems. At half-time, France were 2–1 up thanks to a clever free kick from their playmaker Luka Modrić that caused an own goal and a penalty.

In the second half Kylian was used as a counter-attacking threat. And one that paid off in the fifty-ninth minute. His cross was worked to Paul Pogba on the edge of the area and he smashed it home. 3–1 to France!

Final Flourish

Kylian would not be denied his goal. And it was the best of the lot. He sent a rasping shot past the goalkeeper from more than twenty yards. He was the first teenager to score in a World Cup final in sixty years – the last being Brazil legend Pelé. "Welcome to the club," Pelé later tweeted to Mbappé.

Kylian still felt he was dreaming as France lifted the trophy with gold confetti floating in the air. He kissed the trophy and said he never wanted to let it go.

Championes! Championes! Championes! The French players sang and danced.

Naturally, Kylian was awarded the best young player of the tournament. Emmanuel Macron, the French president, presented him with the award.

"You're a French national hero now," he said. "Thank you."

"My pleasure, sir."

When Kylian and his teammates returned to France they had an open-top bus parade of Paris. Thousands lined the streets to celebrate with them.

But Kylian was not fussed. He wanted to be at home. "Isn't this a bit much?" he said. He wanted to relax and rest, focusing on returning to playing and more trophies. It was just like when he had won the European Under-19 tournament and Monaco's league title.

"Top players aren't happy with what they have already done, so the aim is to win more and more," he said.

BUSINESS AS USUAL

Having won the World Cup at just nineteen and been compared to Pelé, some people thought that Kylian wouldn't have the hunger or desire to keep on scoring goals, making them and winning titles. What was there left to achieve, to work hard for? They didn't know him very well.

Ever since he was a young boy at Bondy he was angered by people saying that his age was a barrier to achieving what he wanted. He felt that in those early days in Monaco too, when the coaches said he was too immature. Kylian's philosophy was "if you're good enough, you're old enough".

Not only did Kylian play like someone who was much older, he spoke with wisdom beyond his years too.

"We can be the best and the world champions, as we are now," he said after the World Cup. "And in four years, you are forgotten, because there is someone else who has arrived and done better than you."

Kylian wanted to build a legacy. So when he returned to Ligue 1 action with Paris Saint-Germain there was no sign that Kylian had lost any of his speed, skill or determination. And so the honours followed again.

In the 2018–19 season the Trophée des Champions was won in August, followed by a stroll to Ligue 1 title by a massive sixteen points. Kylian, now wearing the number 7 shirt as a sign of his rise to senior player status, was the top scorer in the league with thirty-three goals.

All over the world he was seen as an icon. He designed a clothing range with Nike. Madame Tussauds made a waxwork of him. And other players would copy him. The boy who borrowed Cristiano Ronaldo's celebrations had players impersonating him. Liverpool's Trent Alexander-Arnold and

Arsenal's Gabriel Martinelli both copied his goal celebration.

The following season, the coronavirus pandemic hit. The Ligue 1 season was abandoned. PSG were awarded another title, having been twelve points clear of Marseille at the time. Kylian was named top scorer, despite being level on eighteen with Monaco's Wissam Ben Yedder. Kylian edged out Wissam because he had scored more goals from open play. Kylian also had a better goals-per-game ratio, scoring his eighteen goals in twenty games, compared with Wissam's twenty-six.

Still, PSG had failed in 2018–19 to win the Champions League. It was their ultimate goal. They knew there was no point thrashing teams week in and week out in France if they couldn't go to the next level. Kylian was frustrated at their failure and after receiving the player of the season trophy he stunned everyone by saying in his speech: "I've arrived at a first or second turning point of my career. I feel now is the time to have more responsibility. I hope this will be at PSG … or maybe I will go somewhere else."

With no football to play and normal life grinding to a halt because of the virus, Kylian concentrated on charity work. At the start of 2020 Kylian had launched his own charity called Inspired by Kylian Mbappé (IBKM). It supported ninety-eight children from all over Paris to help them achieve their dreams, whatever they were.

"When you are children you have a lot of dreams," he said. "A lot of children have potential but don't have the money to do it. I'm here to help. I will be there for them."

Kylian felt it was really important to use his fame to give something back. He knew he was lucky and that so many were less fortunate than him. This was particularly true as the virus swept through Europe. He donated money to help homeless people get shelter and food with Paris in lockdown.

This wasn't a new idea to Kylian. After the World Cup he donated his entire earnings from the competition – more than £400,000 – to a charity which helps disabled children learn sports.

Kylian was building a legacy off the pitch. But there was still plenty left to do on it. When football returned Kylian and PSG won the French Cup. But Kylian's dream of a Champions League win was dashed again after a special eight-team knockout tournament was organized in Lisbon, Portugal, in

August with no fans allowed. PSG had made it to their first ever final after beating Italian team Atalanta in the quarter-finals and German side RB Leipzig in the semi-finals. But they could not find a way past Bayern Munich, losing 1–0. Kylian had missed a good chance to put PSG in the lead just before Kingsley Coman scored the winner.

Unlike the Champions League, the European Championships in 2020 had been postponed until the following year, meaning Kylian and France would have to wait to see if they could hold both world and European titles at the same time. And the rumours about a move to Real Madrid would not go away.

The boy wonder had never made it a secret that he wanted to win titles in as many of the big leagues as possible. He wanted to win everything, everywhere. Again and again. And few would doubt he could do it.

Timeline

12 July 1998	France win their first World Cup, beating Brazil 3–0 in the final.
20 December 1998	Kylian is born in Bondy, near Paris, France.
2004	Kylian starts to play for AS Bondy, aged six.
2010	Aged eleven, travels to London to have a trial with Chelsea, playing a match against Charlton Athletic.
2011	Joins the famous Clairefontaine academy but continues to play for AS Bondy.
2012	Has a week's trial at Real Madrid.

2012	Joins AS Monaco at age fourteen on a three-year youth contract, rejecting a host of top clubs including Real Madrid, Chelsea, Manchester City, Liverpool, Bayern Munich.
2015	Scores his first goal for Monaco B, the club's reserve team. Scores four goals in fourteen matches for the reserves.
2 December 2015	Makes his first-team debut against SM Caen and becomes the youngest ever Monaco player at sixteen years and 347 days, breaking record set by the legendary Thierry Henry twenty-one years before.
20 February 2016	Scores his first Monaco goal in a 3–1 win over Troyes. At the age of seventeen years and sixty-two days he is the club's youngest ever goalscorer, taking the record from Thierry Henry.

6 March 2016	Signs first professional contract, a three-year deal with Monaco.
15 July 2016	Playing for France in the Under-19 European Championship, Kylian scores his team's second goal against Croatia. He then scores a double against the Netherlands to qualify for the knockouts.
21 July 2016	Almost single-handedly he fires France into the final with two more goals.
24 July 2016	France win the Under-19 European Championship by beating Italy in the final.
14 December 2016	Scores his first hat-trick in a 7–0 hammering of Stade Rennais in the French League Cup.
11 February 2017	Scores his first league hat-trick in a 5–0 win over Metz. At eighteen years and two months he is the youngest ever to score three goals in a Ligue 1 game.

21 February 2017	Scores his first goal in a European competition against Manchester City and in doing so becomes the second youngest French goalscorer in Champions League.
5 March 2017	Scores twice in a 4–0 home Monaco win against FC Nantes. This takes Kylian's Ligue 1 career goal tally to ten, the youngest in thirty years to have achieved it. He has played just 822 minutes of football.
15 March 2017	Monaco beat Manchester 3–1 in the second leg of the Champions League to make it to the quarter-finals. Kylian scores the first goal. It is his eleventh goal in his past eleven matches.
March 2017	Kylian is picked in the France national team squad for matches against Luxembourg and Spain.

25 March	Kylian makes his debut for France against Luxembourg as a substitute. At eighteen years, three months and five days he is the second-youngest ever to play for his country.
11 April 2017	In the quarter-final, Kylian scores a double away to Borussia Dortmund in the first leg to win 3–2. He scores again in the home leg as Monaco win 3–1. Unfortunately Monaco are eliminated by Juventus in the semi-finals, but Kylian scored their only goal.

May 2017 Monaco win the Ligue 1 title. Kylian ends the 2016–17 season with twenty-six goals from forty-four matches in all competitions. He scores fifteen league goals, making him the joint fifth-highest scorer. He is seventh on the list of most assists with eight. He wins the Ligue 1 Young Player of the Year award.

31 August 2017 Kylian gets his first senior international goal in a 3–1 victory over the Netherlands in a World Cup qualifier.

On the same day Paris Saint-Germain announce that they have signed Kylian on loan from Monaco. Kylian will become the second-most expensive player ever.

8 September 2017	Kylian scores on his debut for PSG away to Metz. Four days later he scores again – his first European goal for his new team in the Champions League against Scottish giants Celtic.
6 December 2017	Another record for Kylian. A goal against Bayern Munich in the Champions League gives him ten for the most famous tournament – the youngest player to reach such a mark, at eighteen years and eleven months.
8 May 2018	PSG win the Coupe de France, the most prestigious cup competition in the country, and Kylian scores to see off Les Herbiers VF.
17 May 2018	Kylian is going to the World Cup! He is selected in the squad for the tournament in Russia.

21 June 2018	He makes history in the 1–0 win over Peru in the World Cup. At nineteen he is France's youngest ever goalscorer in the tournament.
30 June 2018	Kylian wins the man of the match award in the 4–3 win over Argentina in the first knockout match at the World Cup. He wins a penalty for Antoine Griezmann and scores two.
July 2018	Kylian is given the famous number 7 shirt by PSG.
8 October 2018	In just thirteen minutes Kylian scores four goals in a 5–0 home victory over Lyon. He also becomes the youngest player (nineteen years and nine months) to score four goals in one game in Ligue 1 for forty-five years.
19 January 2019	Kylian scores a hat-trick in a 9–0 win over Guingamp.

2 March 2019	Against Caen, Kylian scores twice, the second his fiftieth goal for PSG.
May 2019	PSG win the Ligue 1 title. Kylian is named player of the year. He is also the league's top goalscorer with thirty-three.
11 June 2019	Kylian scores his 100th career goal – netting for France against Andorra in a qualifying match for the 2020 European Championship.
3 August 2019	Kylian scores in a 2–1 win over Rennes as PSG win the first title of the new French season: the Trophée des Champions.

22 October 2019	From the substitutes' bench Kylian scores a hat-trick against Club Brugge, a team from Belgium, in the Champions League. It means at the age of twenty years and 306 days he is the youngest to ever score fifteen goals in the competition.
1 May 2020	PSG are named Ligue 1 winners after the coronavirus pandemic forces the abandonment of the season. Kylian is the league's top goalscorer.
July 2020	PSG and Kylian win the French Cup.

Records and Honours

Kylian's Team Honours

France

2018	World Cup
2016	Under-19 European Championship

Paris Saint-Germain

2019–20	Ligue 1, Coupe de la Ligue, Coupe de France
2019	Trophée des Champions
2018–19	Ligue 1
2017–18	Ligue 1, Coupe de la Ligue, Coupe de France

Monaco

2016–17	Ligue 1

Kylian's Individual Honours

Kylian's first award was being named in the team of the tournament in the European Under-19 championship.

He won the Ligue 1 Player of the Year award for the first time for the 2018–19 season.

Three times he has been named the Ligue 1 Young Player of the Year: in 2017, 2018 and 2019. In each of those years he was also named in the Ligue 1 Team of the Year.

He has won five Ligue 1 Player of the Month awards: April 2017, March 2018, February 2019 and February 2021.

After Monaco's 2016–17 season, Kylian was honoured to be named in the Champions League Squad of the Season alongside his idol Cristiano Ronaldo and Lionel Messi. The judges said: "The outstanding young player in an outstanding team of young players. Excellent strike play throughout."

Twice (in 2018 and 2019) Kylian has been named in the FIFPro World XI. FIFPro is the worldwide organisation to help and support footballers.

Kylian has never won the Ballon d'Or (Golden

Ball), the most coveted individual award which recognises the best player in the world. But it is a big ambition. He came seventh in 2017 and fourth in 2018. It is an award dominated by Cristiano Ronaldo and Lionel Messi. Between them they have won eleven of the last twelve.

After his sensational performance in France's World Cup triumph, Kylian was named in the Team of the Tournament and won the Best Young Player award.

Twice he has won the French Player of the Year award, in 2018 and 2019.

He was named in UEFA's Team of the Year in 2018.

In the 2018–19 Ligue 1 season Kylian was top goalscorer with thirty-three goals at a rate of 1.1 per game. In 2019–20 he was top again! This time with eighteen goals at a rate of 0.9 per game.

Kylian's Clubs

Monaco

Club name: *AS Monaco*
Nickname: The Monégasques, the Red and Whites
Short name: Monaco
Founded: 1924
Current manager: Niko Kovač
Current league: Ligue 1
Crest: A gold shield with red and white stripes, topped with a crown

Paris Saint-Germain

Club name: *Paris Saint-Germain*
Nickname: The Parisians, The Red and Blues
Short name: PSG
Founded: 1970
Current manager: Mauricio Pochettino
Current league: Ligue 1
Crest: A blue circle with a red Eiffel Tower in the centre

Appearances and Goals

Monaco

2015–2018
41 appearances, 16 goals

Paris Saint-Germain

2017–present
123 appearances, 106 goals

France

2017–present
42 appearances, 16 goals

Kylian's Favourite Goals

First professional goal

When: 20 February 2016
Playing: Troyes
How it happened: With Troyes trailing 2–1 and pushing high up the pitch for an equaliser, they are caught out by a breakaway. The ball is played across the left of the area to Kylian, whose speed takes him away from the defender and he shoots first time, lifting the ball over the goalkeeper into the centre of the goal.

First European goal

When: 21 February 2017
Playing: Manchester City
How it happened: Playing for Monaco, Kylian is played in behind the Manchester City defence. Defender Nicolás Otamendi thinks he has the eighteen-year-old covered, but he is taken by surprise by the youngster's amazing speed and he is left trailing. Kylian zeroes in on goal and shoots high over the goalkeeper to give Monaco a 2–1 lead.

First goal for France

When: 31 August 2017
Playing: Netherlands
How it happened: This is one of the easiest goals of his career but one of the most important, as it shows he can be a top international player. The Netherlands' defence is all over the place as a cross finds its way to the back post and Kylian makes no mistake, slamming the ball home to give France the lead.

First goal for Paris Saint-Germain

When: 8 September 2017
Playing: Metz
How it happened: On his PSG debut Kylian tries to play an outrageous chip pass to put Neymar in on goal. But the defender cut it out. The ball drops back to Kylian right on the edge of the area and without breaking his stride he smashes a low shot into the goal. All his PSG teammates come to celebrate with him as they know the first goal for a new club is so special.

First goal in the World Cup final

When: 15 July 2018
Playing: Croatia
How it happened: After great tricky play by Lucas Hernandez on the left wing, Kylian is passed the ball twenty-five yards out from goal. He quickly moves into a shooting position and, with his right foot, cuts across the ball with a wicked shot to wrong-foot the goalkeeper to make history. He runs away and his mobbed by his teammates before he can even finish his trademark celebration.

Did You Know?

Kylian is very active on social media. He has 5.9 million followers on Twitter and more than 50 million followers on Instagram! He uses his accounts to remind his followers of the importance of family, to highlight good causes, such as the Black Lives Matter campaign, or during the coronavirus to remind fans to wear face masks.

Kylian is not just famous for his footballing brilliance. He is famous for being wise beyond his years. Benjamin Mendy, his France teammate and former Monaco teammate, has nicknamed him 'my little Obama' after the American President Barack Obama. Why? Because he listens carefully to questions and gives thoughtful answers.

Between the ages of six and eleven Kylian attended a centre for performing arts in Paris, where he learned to sing, read music and play the flute.

Kylian can speak Spanish. He started taking lessons in 2019 and is known to speak fluently in the language with Neymar in the PSG dressing room. Neymar learned when he was at Barcelona.